His expression was grim, his eyes flat. She recognized this side of him. The way he dissociated and focused only on his duty—never on what he actually wanted.

"If I let you go, if I pretend this never happened, there is no guarantee you do not change your mind. No guarantee that the child should not come of age and find out and cause an uproar. We must be married and make the child legitimate. There is no alternative if that child is mine."

It hurt, because perhaps deep down underneath so many protections she'd at least wished a *little* his showing up here meant he'd changed his mind, or perhaps that he cared for her in some small way.

But no, it was about duty. Potential scandal. It was about protecting his crown at any and all costs.

She could not win in this, no, but she could at least wipe that superior look off his face.

"If the *children* are yours, you mean."

"Excuse me?"

"It is not *a* child, Diamandis. It is children. We are having twins."

Secrets of the Kalyva Crown

It started with a royal revenge...

Banished following the execution of his parents,
Lysias has spent years plotting revenge on the
surviving royal of a bloody coup, King Diamandis.
Now justice is *finally* within reach, as he has hired
someone to pose as the king's long-lost sister...

King Diamandis believed he was the sole
surviving member of his royal family. Ruling with
an ironclad fist was the only way he knew how to
continue their legacy. Until his whole world is tilted
on its axis by his supposed sister's royal return...

Soon, both of their carefully constructed plans and
lives will be thrown into complete disarray—by
love!

Read Lysias and Al's story in
Hired for His Royal Revenge

And read Diamandis and Katerina's story
Pregnant at the Palace Altar

Both available now!

Lorraine Hall

PREGNANT AT THE PALACE ALTAR

HARLEQUIN
PRESENTS

HARLEQUIN®
PRESENTS™

Recycling programs
for this product may
not exist in your area.

ISBN-13: 978-1-335-73947-6

Pregnant at the Palace Altar

Harlequin Enterprises ULC
22 Adelaide St. West, 41st Floor
Toronto, Ontario M5H 4E3, Canada
www.Harlequin.com

Printed in U.S.A.

Lorraine Hall is a part-time hermit and full-time writer. She was born with an old soul and her head in the clouds, which, it turns out, is the perfect combination to spend her days creating thunderous alpha heroes and the fierce, determined heroines who win their hearts. She lives in a potentially haunted house with her soulmate and rambunctious band of hermits-in-training. When she's not writing romance, she's reading it.

Books by Lorraine Hall

Harlequin Presents

The Prince's Royal Wedding Demand

Secrets of the Kalyva Crown
Hired for His Royal Revenge

For Soraya. Thank you for your boundless enthusiasm.

CHAPTER ONE

As FAR AS King Diamandis Agonas was concerned, royal weddings were a royal pain. His only comfort in being involved in the planning of this one was that it was not his own wedding.

That would be a disaster.

But being the king while his sister—the long-lost princess who'd only been returned to them earlier this year—got married was proving more challenging than he would have preferred.

In any other circumstances, he would have labeled the whole affair a debacle. First, Zandra and her betrothed had run off to Athens to get married months ago and then the announcement of her pregnancy had brought about the need to move up the date of the royal wedding ceremony, and Diamandis had found himself uncharacteristically bending over backward for his sister.

He blamed it on the fact he'd considered her dead for nearly twenty years. What man wouldn't want to make up for lost time? What king wouldn't want to give his sister, the princess, all she desired, and all that was befitting a Kalyvan princess?

He eyed her now, moving around his office. She was

not a *sitter*, this woman. Not the placid, obedient princess she might have been if she'd grown up in the palace. If their family had not been murdered in a bloody attempt at a political coup twenty years ago.

Instead, the monarchy had managed to withstand the attack and Diamandis had been proclaimed king in the wake of his parents' and brothers' deaths.

Zandra, with the help of a servant boy, had somehow escaped, lost her memory in the process, and grown up on the streets of Athens as an orphan. That same servant boy—Lysias Balaskas, who was now a billionaire and Zandra's husband—had returned her to Kalyva earlier this year.

So Zandra was home where she belonged. She was his sister, proven by DNA tests, and yet it was like his sister was two different people to him: the toddler he'd known for the first four years of her life, and now this woman, whom he didn't understand and couldn't begin to make sense of. So open and sweet, with a backbone that was giving him a headache.

Yet she was his sister—he knew this elementally—and he loved her.

No matter how she puzzled, irritated and defied him.

Because her eyes were the same—whether she was the four-year-old poking him in the throat, or this woman saying things that nearly knocked him off his feet.

"When I was in Athens, you'll never guess who I saw." Luckily, she did not pause and make him guess. "Katerina."

Diamandis did not stiffen. He did not allow himself to be caught off guard by *anything* anymore. Or so he told himself. His former assistant had caught him off guard more times than he cared to count.

He did not allow his mind to conjure up images of her. She had fled in the middle of the night, leaving only a note, and so she was as good as dead to him.

At least that was what he told himself whenever the memory of her popped up. He tried to convince himself this was simply because she was the best assistant he'd ever had and every attempt at replacement had failed dismally.

He did not allow himself to think of *that night*. In *this* office. The exquisite perfection of her and all that could not be.

Ever.

"What does this have to do with the wedding preparations?" Diamandis asked, stiffly.

His curtness did not deter Zandra, but then very few things did. "It doesn't, but I think I may have solved your mystery of why she up and left."

"Oh?" Diamandis had his own suspicions, but they were ones he would never share with his sister. Or anyone.

"I saw her in the baby store. With a belly bigger than mine."

Diamandis did not move. He did not hear whatever Zandra said next. Everything was simply a buzzing in his ears.

A belly bigger than mine.

"I suppose that's why she left," Zandra said after she'd rambled on about something. "Heaven knows I wouldn't want to be growing a human while suffering under *your* beck and call."

"What?"

Zandra slid her hand over her rounded belly as if that was the answer.

It *couldn't* be the answer.

"It is odd, though," Zandra said, tapping her chin as if deep in thought.

"What is?" Diamandis said between gritted teeth, beyond irritated that his frustration was leaking through when *nothing* about Katerina Floros mattered to him. *Nothing.* Not why she'd left or what state she was currently in.

She had left. The end.

"She didn't seem to want to see me, so I didn't approach her and ask. Of course every pregnancy and woman is different, or so I've read, but she seemed to be even farther along than *me*. Considering how you had her working practically around the clock, I'm not sure how she found the time to become pregnant while working for you." Then all the casual indifference turned sharp, her dark gaze pinning his. "I don't suppose *you* had anything to do with it."

"With what?"

She rolled her eyes. "Please tell me you're not the deadbeat father of her baby, Diamandis."

Diamandis straightened and stared down at his sister. "I am the king of Kalyva."

"So?"

She really was the most impossible creature. He did not understand why Lysias didn't…*do* something about her.

Or why you, the king and her brother, don't.

But that was neither here nor there. "I am *not* a deadbeat. Nor the father of Katerina's child. She left in the dark of night all those months ago and I have not seen her since."

"Yes, six months ago. About the time she likely found out she was pregnant. It just seems likely that the two events are connected."

"I assure you *I* had nothing to do with whatever predicament she finds herself in."

Zandra shrugged, her hands resting over her own rounded belly. Diamandis refused to let his imagination create a version of Katerina in that state.

He was a *king*. If the regrettable night of passion had led to a child, his efficient assistant would have informed him and requested compensation. They would have dealt with the problem at hand. There would have been no cause to run away.

To do so would be foolish and shortsighted, and Katerina had never been any of those things, even in the aftermath of their one...*hiccup*.

He preferred to refer to it as that.

"I have much to do, Zandra. Was there anything else you wished to discuss?"

She eyed him carefully, and he did not know what his sister was searching for, or whether she found it. She moved forward, brushing a kiss across his cheek. "Nothing else, Diamandis. I will see you at dinner." Then she departed.

Diamandis stood exactly where he was. He told himself that this information changed nothing. He would go on about his day as planned.

He pressed the button on his desk that would alert his assistant that his presence was required.

While he waited, Diamandis stood staring blindly

out the window. It was impossible. He was sure it was impossible.

But unfortunately, Zandra was correct. Katerina's life as his assistant *had* been demanding. When would she have had time to go off and engage in some affair? He would have heard about it, known about it.

So there was only one course of action now, no matter how impossible this all seemed.

When his new assistant *finally* appeared, Diamandis didn't look at him. He simply said, "I will be flying to Athens. Make the arrangements. Immediately."

"The brave, courageous prince stood between the princess and the dangerous dragon, and with one mighty swipe he saved the princess from certain death!"

Katerina Floros *hated* this story, but the children in her classroom loved it. The illustration of the prince slaying the dragon was just gruesome enough to be titillating for the four-year-old set, the tale of a prince and princess and a dragon just imaginative enough to fill many of them with the typical childhood awe.

Any awe Katerina might have had at royalty and glittering dresses and fearsome princes had long since fallen prey to disillusionment. Instead, she felt sorry for the dragon. *He* likely had been minding his own business, doing his job, only to have the prince swoop in and ruin everything.

The children made excited conversation about the illustration, as per usual, and then Katerina hurried them through their end-of-day routines. Parents began to arrive to pick up their children after long days at work.

It was hard for Katerina to believe she would be one of them soon—rushing about, working and parenting.

She liked to believe she'd be the flawless, unbothered mother with big smiles and hugs. She had a bad feeling she'd be the harried one, bustling around, begging for the children to *please* move along faster because they had places to be. But that was still a little way off... though it was getting ever closer.

Once all the children had been picked up, and most of the staff had gone, Katerina collected her things. Her boss—the director of the childcare center and Katerina's personal savior—joined her.

"Won't be long for you now." Fifi gave her stomach a little pat. Katerina *hated* people touching her belly, but Fifi had been a godsend for giving her a job and time off to attend doctor's appointments, and Katerina didn't have it in her to ask her not to do that.

They walked outside together into a cloudy evening, offering small talk and then goodbyes. In her head, Katerina was praying her little junker of a car would start. When it did, she offered a little thank-you to the universe and then drove home.

She parked on the street in front of her apartment complex in a questionable neighborhood on the outskirts of Athens. It was not a palace. It wasn't even the glittering beach bungalow she'd grown up in on the island nation of Kalyva. It was, in fact, a hovel, at best. But it was *her* hovel, which she paid for with money *she* earned. Because she *refused* to follow in her mother's footsteps any more than she already had.

She'd make her own way. She'd love her child, and if that meant struggling for money in the beginning, so be it. There would be love—and that was better than secrets and money.

Katerina would make it work. She always did.

There was a crowd a way down the street, and though Katerina was curious, she kept her head down and walked into her building. Nothing good came from gathered crowds—this she knew.

So she walked up the stairs, cursing her third-story apartment as she did every evening when her stomach felt particularly heavy and her feet positively ached. She was starving, exhausted, and couldn't wait to eat dinner in the bathtub as had become an indulgent ritual every night after work.

She unlocked the door, stepped inside and froze. There was a strange scent in the air. Something very... masculine. Her heart seized there in her chest and she reached for the door behind her with one hand. In the other, she held her keys in between her fingers, ready to defend herself in whatever way she could.

But even as she did so she knew there was no defense against this.

He was here. In her apartment. On her raggedy, sunken couch cushion. She had done everything to make her place cozy and cheerful, but in the shadow of *him* it seemed dim, dirty. Shameful.

The king of Kalyva sat on her couch. Her former boss.

And more.

Her hands slowly dropped from their fighter's stance to her stomach, as if she could hide that fact from him. She had a lie ready. She'd hold on to that lie with all she had, and yet...

The sight of him still stole her breath. It seemed time away had stripped her of all those old tricks she'd once employed in order not to react outwardly to the man.

The king.

She could still hear herself breathlessly call him "my king" that one stupid night she'd forgotten every promise she'd ever made to herself. All because this man had kissed her.

All because she was a *fool*. The fool her mother had always told her she'd be when a handsome, powerful man took what he wanted—and *you* wanted.

She should have known he'd be here. She'd thought she'd managed to hide from Princess Zandra in the baby store the other day, but she should have known. Should have known the princess was kind enough to have pretended not to see her as Katerina had clearly not wanted to be seen.

But not kind enough to keep it to herself.

Diamandis unfolded himself, the height and breadth of him seeming to block out the sad light of the fluorescent fixture behind him. His dark hair was cut in the same ruthless style it always was, his dark brows and eyes as severe as ever. His muscular frame was enhanced by one of his requisite black suits. She knew he thought it practical and that it made him look intimidating to all who would oppose him, but it was little more than repressed mourning, because he had never dealt with any of the tragedies that had befallen him.

She knew this all too well, and it was a large part of why she'd run the moment she'd found herself pregnant. Diamandis did not deal with anything that did not suit the narrative he had created for his life—and she could not even hate him for that after the way he'd lost his family and had somehow kept his kingdom from crumbling. At *fourteen*.

She hadn't trusted herself to be strong in the face of him, and she would have needed an immense amount of strength. He had spent *years* telling everyone who would listen that, if he had the choice, he'd never marry, never have children. So this little *lapse* would not fit into his plans.

And *she* would pay the price.

A price she knew intimately. And she had no wish to pass any of that on to her children the way her own mother had done.

So Katerina had left. Disappeared. *Run.* Determined to handle all of this on her own. She had always been on her own, even when at the whims of her mother, so it had seemed the only course of action. She'd been certain he wouldn't think twice about her disappearance.

He'd forget *all* about her, and never, ever know. Or care.

She was saving them both, really.

But now he was here. Now he likely knew. And what power did she have against a king?

You will have to find some, Katerina. She held her hands more tightly around her stomach.

"Has it really been so long that you've forgotten protocol, Ms. Floros?" he said, and she recognized that cool, detached tone and the way he said her formal name with those clipped vowels. It hid a fury most people never guessed at. But she knew.

She knew all too well.

He studied her, encased in all that ice he wielded so well. "You are supposed to curtsy in the presence of your king."

CHAPTER TWO

SHE DID NOT CURTSY. Diamandis did not know if this was some act of defiance—which he did not understand—or whether in her state she would struggle to make such a movement. He seemed to remember his mother walking about the castle when heavy with child, complaining bitterly about her size, her discomfort, then, upon seeing him, flash a smile and bring him into a hug he was far too old for and tell him it was always worth it.

He did not care for memories of his mother, and he could admit that this soured his already less than controlled disposition.

"What are you doing here, Diamandis?"

He raised an eyebrow at the cheek of her using his first name without any honorific. But she didn't wither. She'd always been an effective and efficient assistant, capable of hiding in the shadows and also capable of standing up to him when it was necessary.

But today she'd picked the wrong moment to stand up to him.

"An interesting question. I imagine you have some ideas."

She rested her hand on her belly, which was round and lush. The moment he'd seen her his hands had itched to reach out and feel the swell of it under the loose, gauzy fabric she wore. Her dark, curly hair was pulled back, but quite a few strands had fallen out and wisped around her face. She wore no makeup and did not resemble the slim, efficient assistant he'd once known.

Which seemed to change his body's reaction to her not at all. She had long been a problem. A temptation. He'd convinced himself he was immune, that he was *better* than his baser urges, because his entire life was pledged in service to his kingdom. There was no room for his wants.

That night had been a failure in so many ways, but he'd at the very least convinced himself he'd exorcised such foolish lust.

Even when he could still taste her. Even when her "my king" still echoed in his head.

He curled his hand into a fist, needing something to remind him of his purpose. He must not touch her. He needed to determine if she was pregnant with *his* child, because clearly she was indeed pregnant.

He did not want a wife, a queen. He did not want children. Finding Zandra might have fulfilled him on a personal level, but it had also taken a great weight off his shoulders. He did not have to worry about heirs.

He knew what it was to be the heir. It was why he was still alive.

No matter how much time he'd spent wishing he'd been the one murdered.

"My sister comes home from a shopping trip to Athens with news that my former assistant, who ran away in the dead of night, is gallivanting about Athens, pregnant. More pregnant even than my sister herself, which seemed odd timing to Zandra, since she did not think you'd have had time to become so when you were working for me."

"The princess does have a curious, inquisitive mind," Katerina returned. Her tone was cool. Her hands were still, but her eyes...

Her alluring green eyes had always told another story than the masks she wore so beautifully. He hadn't always wanted to uncover that story. Had actively avoided seeing beneath her composed demeanor.

Except for that one night.

"You know why I am here, Katerina."

"I do not, Diamandis. While I can understand why you might be under the impression that our one...*encounter* might have caused my current situation, that my entire life in Kalyva was spent being a slave to you, you are mistaken. I had my own life, and I lived it. Now I am happily living it in Athens with my husband, who happens to be the father of this child."

He was surprised—not by the information, but by the blatant lie. Did she really think he hadn't looked into her life over the past six months on his way here? "So. You've married?"

"Yes."

Diamandis took a moment to try and decide whether she thought him *stupid*, or whether she was just very, very desperate. He did not understand desperation, did not understand this place or her, so surely she thought him stupid.

Some people thought worse of him than that, he supposed. Still, it grated. Particularly as she'd been privy to much information few other royal staff members were. "I am supposed to believe this ludicrous story? You forget that I knew your every move, and still do."

She sniffed. "Impossible."

"I am the king, Katerina."

"You are *a* king, Diamandis. One of many that exist in this big world."

She had often been forthright with him in her position as his assistant—but she had known her place. She had been adept at using the appropriate tone. Usually. This was not forthright and it was not measured.

This was defiance. He looked around the hovel she had tried to make into a home, and he could not understand this game. "There is not one shred of evidence that a man lives here. There is no record of a marriage, and as we stand here and discuss it, no dutiful husband returns to make you dinner."

"He works nights," she returned with a sniff, still standing there by the door as if she might make a break for it.

Surely she knew there was no escape now?

"Does he? Then show me, Katerina. Prove this union to me."

She stood there, her arm curved around her belly as though she held the weight of it in her hands. She said nothing.

Which was answer enough. "Ah, you cannot." He shook his head. "You will return to Kalyva with me at once. If you continue to insist I am not the father, I am afraid a test must be done."

"Why?" she demanded, something in her slumping, and Diamandis did not like watching how that fierce light of defiance seemed to dim. He had always admired her backbone. Her strength. She had never been afraid of him, even when he had wanted her to be.

"What do you mean *why*? We were together and reckless. I am sure you remember."

She lifted her chin and looked at some point on the grimy wall behind him. "Not really," she said loftily.

But the telltale flush that spread across her cheeks told another story, and it aroused him, when he could not afford such a distraction.

Ever again.

There was a child. His child. And he had to fix this problem before it became unfixable. "You lie, Katerina."

She slumped again, leaning back against the door. She looked tired and her eyes were growing wet when her gaze met his again.

"You do not want children, Diamandis. You have always been very clear on your stance on that. Why take me back to Kalyva? Why run tests? You do not want this, even if you are the father."

"Is this why you ran?" He knew it must be, in part. Or she would have run the night after they were together, not a few weeks later.

She did not answer. She just looked at him with a hopeless kind of expression that had his insides twisting into hard knots. He supposed it was some kind of guilt, though he could not see how he had done anything wrong.

She had not told him. *She* had not given him an opportunity to have a say in the matter. She'd simply fled. She did not get to make him feel guilty now.

"I could have you arrested. I could have you taken, forcefully, back to Kalyva."

"I'm sure you could."

She sounded so tired. She had likely worked all day at the daycare center that sent her monthly paychecks. She had walked up three flights of stairs all to rest her head in this cramped, uncomfortable space, and she would still refuse to return to Kalyva? Where she would be taken care of, regardless of his wants when it came to children?

She made *no* sense.

Still, while he *could* have her arrested under Kalyva law thanks to a treaty with the Greek government, he much preferred a peaceful capitulation. "I am a fair man, Katerina. It does not have to be all about me."

She snorted. "Since when?"

He ignored this derision. "What is it you desire? Surely not this sad little apartment, and a job that underpays and no doubt underappreciates you? Surely not a life in Athens when you could come home and—"

"And what? Be the butt of every joke? Be fodder for gossip? Watch my child grow to be whispered about and called the king's *bastard*." The fight, the fire was back in her eyes and in her posture. She radiated an anger he had not anticipated. "No, Diamandis. I will not sentence any of us to such a fate. Maybe this life is not as nice and fine as the one you are used to, but it is respectable. It will allow my chi—"

"*Our* child."

She stopped at that. As if her words had dried up and she had nothing more to say. He struggled to find his own.

Our *child*. His child. An heir.

"I have no wish to return to Kalyva to gossip and cruelty," Katerina said on little more than a whisper.

"You do not wish to have a wife or a child. Let us leave it at that, Diamandis. I will ask you for nothing if you stay away from me. Surely this is fair to both of us."

"I am afraid this will not do, Katerina. You will return to Kalyva, and you will begin preparations."

"Preparations for *what*?"

"For our wedding, of course."

Katerina was certain she was dreaming. There was no other possible explanation for this. Only it wasn't a dream. It was a nightmare.

Perhaps when she'd worked for him she had sometimes allowed her fantasies to wander perilously close to *caring*—at least when it came to the man he was underneath the crown and the trauma responses—but she had always known a happy ending was not on the cards. That he had found her attractive had been shocking enough, and she had not dealt with that realization wisely.

So she had to deal with these events wisely. Because it wasn't about her. It was about…

Our child.

He had said ours, and her heart… Oh, it was traitorous.

"I cannot marry you, Diamandis."

"Getting married solves all of your concerns."

"Hardly. The pit vipers in your court will still deem this pregnancy illegitimate. Conceived out of wedlock. A stain on the monarchy." She couldn't bear it. Would not allow it.

If she had to run away again, she would. Farther this time. She could go to England or America or anywhere Diamandis couldn't reach her.

"We will concoct a story. Lysias and Zandra had an unsanctioned Athens wedding, why not us?"

"Diamandis, you are the *king*." It felt a bit like going back in time, back to when she had been his assistant, and in a way, his conscience. Because he tended to listen to his old, stuffy, aristocratic advisers, but when she'd voiced concern, when she'd reminded him that tradition had its place but the world was also changing, sometimes he'd listened.

"And due to some health issues, we needed to conduct ourselves secretly," he continued, as if she hadn't spoken at all. Another reminder of the past. "The pregnancy complicated your health, so you remained in Athens under a doctor's care while I returned to Kalyva. It was imperative we did not let the public in on such events so you could recuperate in peace. We could not be married in their eyes until you were well enough."

"Who will believe this?" And why was she even entertaining such an absurd possibility? She would not marry him. She would not…

"Everyone. Because I will make certain it becomes the truth."

Katerina knew he believed this. He might even be able to make it work by sheer force of will. That was the power of Diamandis. It was hard and it was implacable. He had been forced to build himself up into such a man after everything that had happened when he'd been little more than a boy.

She couldn't start thinking about *that*, though, or she might soften as she so often had as his assistant. "I am still as common as common comes, and you cannot make that different. You cannot change the narrative around you marrying your former assistant."

"Lysias was a servant boy. They have taken to him well enough."

"Oh, the billionaire who saved the princess's life? Shocking that they would be supportive of the princess marrying such a man."

She saw impatience simmer behind his eyes and yet he stayed perfectly still. "You are giving this too much thought."

"And you are not giving it enough."

These were lines they had said to each other often when she'd been in his employ—but in the reverse. She had always wanted him to…loosen up. Katerina had often seen ways he might make himself more human to his subjects. *She* had once been the one to accuse him of thinking too much.

And he had always accused her of not thinking of the *implications*.

How on earth had their positions switched? How had she ended up *here*?

"You will be an effective queen, Katerina."

"I have no desire to be queen." No desire to be *effective* for him again. A tool to be trotted out when he saw fit and nothing more.

"And we have proven that we are compatible. In and out of the bedroom."

"What bedroom, Diamandis?" she said tiredly, because they had hardly had some grand love affair. They'd had a night of foolishly shared grief. On his desk. In his office.

She could not travel back to that night in her mind

or she would remember too many things that were best lost to time.

"Ah, so you do remember."

She sighed. She was too tired for this ridiculous conversation. For this. For him. To fight her own reaction to him as he stalked over to her and stood above her, glaring down at her with that dark gaze that at one time she'd known how to *pretend* didn't affect her.

"I said no," she said, trying to sound firm. Like she had in the old days when she'd stood up to him. "I will not go back. I will not marry you. The answer is *no*."

"It was not a question, Katerina. Your king has commanded you, and so you will obey." He waited a beat, but she could not control her fast breaths enough to speak in that pause.

"Would you like me to help you pack?" he asked with that condescending I-am-the-king smile that had made her angry even when she'd been his assistant.

"You haven't packed a bag once in your life, Diamandis."

"And you have excellent skills in that department," he offered.

The worst part was that she had no doubt he thought that was a compliment. He thought he was being kind. And that broke apart what little control she was holding on to.

Because he had all the money and power in this situation, and she did not understand why he would use it for this purpose. She was giving him what he wanted—a chance to be free of the children he did not want. She was giving them both what they wanted by getting out and keeping the secret to her grave. So she could not understand this or him.

"Why, Diamandis?" she asked, eyes filling with tears. "You do not want me. You do not want children. I have given you an out. Why won't you take it?"

His expression was grim, his eyes flat. She recognized this side of him. The way he disassociated and focused only on his duty—never on what he actually wanted. "If I let you go, if I pretend this never happened, there is no guarantee that you will not change your mind. No guarantee that the child should not come of age and find out and cause an uproar. We must be married and make the child legitimate. There is no alternative if that child is mine."

It hurt, because perhaps deep down, a part of her had wished that his showing up here meant he'd changed his mind, or that perhaps he cared for her in some small way.

But no. It was about duty. Potential scandal. It was about protecting his crown at any and all costs.

She could not win in this, but she could at least wipe that superior look off his face.

"If the *children* are yours, you mean."

"Excuse me?"

"It is not *a* child, Diamandis. It is children. We are having twins."

CHAPTER THREE

DIAMANDIS FELT AS though that word echoed around in his head as a sort of cymbal crash. Over and over. *Twins, twins, twins.*

Two babies. Two children. And Katerina.

"You look a little pale," Katerina said with a thinly veiled smirk. "Perhaps you should sit down."

He swallowed and straightened his shoulders. It was a surprise, yes, but hardly the blow she wanted it to be. Diamandis had been through too much to be knocked fully off course by this.

Twins.

He did not clear his throat, though it felt clogged and tight. He was still able to speak clearly and forcefully, at least in his own head. "If there is anything you need from this…place, I suggest you collect it."

"Are you going to sic your guards on me if I do not?" she returned.

"Of course not, *glyko mou.* I will carry you myself." And then he smiled, because he would carry her if he had to.

He'd do whatever he had to do. He was the king and had been since he was fourteen. Since he'd had to order the blood of his loved ones to be cleaned from their bedroom floors. Since he'd realized after that first dark year that some of his advisers had, in fact, acted in their own best interests—not the kingdom's or his.

So nothing deterred him anymore. Nothing got in his way. He had his father's legacy to uphold. He could not be beloved as King Youkilis had been—too many mistakes had already been made—but he could keep his country safe and prosperous. He could make certain his behavior was above reproach so no one ever had reason to believe him less than his father's dutiful son and heir.

Katerina had been a mistake. He could blame it on the emotional upheaval of finding out Zandra was alive, or he could take responsibility for his actions.

Diamandis always took responsibility. So, though he had no desire for a queen or family, she would become his. There was no question. The child—*children*—she carried were his. There were no other possible outcomes.

What he wanted or did not want had never signified before. They would not now.

"Do you need a countdown, Katerina?"

She held his gaze for what felt like hours. He saw the myriad greens that leaned toward blue and gray in different lights; the elegant curve of her neck; the soft, honeyed skin over which he'd once run his hands.

It still echoed within him. Between them…the way she had fallen apart in his arms as though she had yearned for him exactly as he had yearned for her since that very first meeting.

He was not alone in this torturous want, he knew, simply by the color rising on her cheeks. He wished that were some kind of comfort.

"I cannot understand your reluctance."

"Reluctance?" She groaned in disgust. "You are delusional. This is not reluctance. It is refusal."

"We will be married, Katerina, and while you seem to view that as some kind of tragedy, I assure you that you will want for nothing, as queen."

"Except a warm, loving home and privacy," she returned.

He had once had that warm, loving home. His childhood was nothing but memories of his parents' love, his family's devotion. But these things did not matter, regardless of how good they might feel. These things were as fragile as glass and could be taken away by any person's whims.

So, no, he did not plan to fill his home with *love.*

Twins, twins, twins.

"You get along quite well with my sister. I'm sure the two of you can forge some kind of friendship as you enter motherhood together. You may fill your part of the palace with as much warmth and love as you so wish."

This did not wipe the frown off her face. The downward curve only settled deeper, when it was a good and kind point, all in all.

"Do you recall what I said to you when your plan was to throw Lysias in a dungeon the minute he stepped on Kalyva soil?"

Diamandis did not care to think about the days that had led up to learning Zandra was indeed his long-lost sister. At the time, Diamandis had been certain his former best friend had returned to Kalyva with an imposter, meant to hurt Diamandis. Now, months later, he felt justified in *most* of his treatment of Lysias, who had not returned with Zandra out of the goodness of his heart, but with revenge on his mind. But somehow love had changed that for Lysias, though Diamandis did not know why any man who'd been through what they had could be felled by *love*. In the end, Lysias had fallen for Zandra and given up on revenge.

Now, somehow, they were a family…as Zandra kept reminding him, no matter how much Diamandis withdrew into himself.

He looked at Katerina, knowing she would now have to be part of it all, knowing it would be harder—but even more necessary—to withdraw from her.

His duty was to Kalyva, and Kalyva alone. So he had heeded her advice at the time and not thrown Lysias in the dungeons.

"You said it would be seen as the action of a cruel, lifeless robot, which I was not," he returned stiffly, because she had been right about the situation and that fact still burned. He wished *cruel, lifeless robot* was more within his reach than his conscience ever let it be.

"I was wrong," Katerina said, looking at him with an anger he'd never seen there in her eyes. "You *are* a cruel, lifeless robot. I don't want anything or anyone to ever hurt my children. I know you will. This alone proves it."

She had never been afraid to stand up to him in the years she'd worked for him, but she'd also never stabbed such a dagger into his heart. "I do not hurt people, Ms. Floros. As king, it is my job to protect them."

As his family had not been protected. And now, somehow, he had family once again. The one thing he did not want. For he would never be worthy of it.

"You speak of violence, Diamandis, but it doesn't take a bloody coup or an attack to hurt people. You can hurt them by not listening to them. By ignoring their needs. You can hurt them by—"

"This is your last chance," he said, struggling with the temper he knew was one of his worst traits. He'd learned to control it over the years, but it was a constant battle, particularly when someone was being so unreasonable—someone he had once respected before she'd betrayed him.

"My last chance for what?" she returned tartly.

"A civil, voluntary arrangement. If you do not come with me now, you will lose your job, this apartment, and the chance to have anything else. When those children are born, they will be taken from you. I will make certain of it. This is not my wish, but if you twist my arm, I will make it happen. They are the heirs." *God help them.* "They are mine. This is the *only* course of action."

Her breathing became ragged, but she did not fall apart. She did not beg his forgiveness or jump to act. She simply stared at him with hatred in her beautiful eyes.

He hated that a black, oily emotion roiled through him—one he refused to examine. "I will be in the car. You have fifteen minutes to make your choice." And with that he strode out of the apartment.

He had done the right thing. For his kingdom. For his legacy.

Whatever came next was Katerina's choice, and he would not feel guilt over that.

He refused to.

Katerina stood stock-still and in place for long ticking minutes after Diamandis exited. She could scarcely catch a breath. She couldn't think.

He had threatened everything. He had left her with some choice but it was no choice at all. Because he was a king, and she was a no one.

The only way to be someone, darling, is to align yourself to the right man.

Oh, how her mother would love this. Marrying a king. She'd likely crawl out of the woodwork and Katerina would have to deal with her, too.

How could this have all come crashing down so quickly? All because of a chance meeting at a baby store. If she'd stayed in her lane—poking around secondhand shops—she never would have seen the princess. Diamandis would have never known.

She wanted to wallow in the what-ifs, spend time self-flagellating over her mistakes, but Diamandis had given her fifteen minutes, and as much as she might have enjoyed thwarting him, she knew him. She had been his personal assistant for too long not to understand at least in part how his mind worked and what had shaped him to think that way.

He did not want a queen or children, but he would suffer through anything he didn't want if he could avoid a scandal that might put a stain on the throne. He considered this his duty to his long-dead parents, and that was a duty he viewed as sacred.

So, yes, he would not be above getting her removed from her job, her apartment. He would not balk at taking her children from her, because in his mind there was only one right way: to have control over his heirs, and, for the sake of his royal subjects, the respectability of being married to their mother.

He had truly given her no choice, and if she faltered or hesitated, she would pay the price. She'd have to wait until they were back in Kalyva to wallow in her poor choices.

From *that* night on.

She went to her room and packed a few things, but she'd taken very little with her when she'd fled the palace and Kalyva. She'd bought even less since building a life in Athens. Still, she packed the few things she'd bought for the baby, her maternity clothes and toiletries. She gave her apartment one last look.

She could not say she'd enjoyed her time here. It had felt necessary, not fun or independent. But it had been *hers*.

And now nothing would be.

She was tired and hungry. Weak and devastated. If she forced herself to look on the bright side, a stay in the palace would mean a comfortable bed and good food and someone else taking care of the details for a little bit.

Maybe once she rested, she'd have a clearer head and be able to come up with a way to get around Diamandis's will. She had talked him out of things before. She only needed time to talk him out of things again.

She turned away from the life she'd built and walked down the stairs to the sidewalk. The commotion earlier must have been over the sleek car on the street, but it had since been cleared. The driver stood outside the car, as no doubt Diamandis would not risk being seen. He was not well known outside of Kalyva, but Greece was close enough that you never knew when someone might recognize you from old news stories about murdered royals.

The driver opened the door for her as she approached. "Christos," she greeted with a small smile.

Clearly Diamandis did not know that his driver-slash-bodyguard and his partner had been the ones to help her get off Kalyva without detection. "So good to see you again."

He bobbed his head. "And you, Ms. Floros."

She turned to the car and looked to the spacious back seat where Diamandis sat.

"If your ridiculous story is not believed by all and sundry, I will take my children and run and you will never, *ever* find me. I will not tolerate whispers, gossip, or ridicule for my children."

"Nor will I, Katerina."

She knew that was true to an extent, but she also knew he didn't fully understand how people could twist things. How whispers could follow you, ruin you. Which brought her to her second condition.

"If my mother appears in any context, you will refuse to let her anywhere near me."

Diamandis raised an eyebrow, and she knew this would give him reason to poke into the matter. Of course, he must know a little about her mother from the extensive background check he'd run before he'd hired her, but he likely thought himself above and immune to Ghavriella Floros's machinations.

Katerina wasn't so sure.

"As you wish," he replied, unbothered. "Get inside the car, Katerina. There is much to do."

Katerina gave one last backward glance at her apartment. At her life in Athens. No matter what happened next, she knew she would not be able to come back here. The door was closing on this chapter of her life.

But so many doors had closed on her—some by her choosing but most by someone else's. She knew how to do this. She knew how to start over. She knew how to fight, and she would always, *always* fight for her children.

So she slid inside the car, not yet resigned to being a queen but determined to make the best choices for her children.

CHAPTER FOUR

IT WAS QUITE late by the time they returned to Kalyva and the palace. Katerina had slept most of the way, groggily moving from car to boat before falling asleep once more.

Diamandis should have been making arrangements or working, but instead he'd found himself watching her, monitoring the slow rise and fall of her breathing, cataloging every change in her now that she was pregnant.

And realizing how much he'd observed her before without fully realizing that was what he'd been doing all the years she'd worked for him. He certainly did not know or care what Tomás's eyelashes looked like against his cheek, or how exhaustion might look on any of his assistants' faces.

Except Katerina's. As it had after long weeks around special events and committee meetings. As it did now.

When the boat docked at his private royal pier, he briefly considered staying right here until she woke up on her own. She needed a bed, though. Comfort. And likely a meal. There was no way she'd been taking appropriate care of herself if she'd been working and walking up and down those apartment stairs every day.

He fought off the anger, icing it away into its compartment. There were things he could control and things he couldn't. The past was one of the few things that fell into the *couldn't* category.

The future, and how she was taken care of, was well within his control, and that was all that could matter. He eyed the swell of her stomach. Children. *His* children. For a moment, he had the foreign impulse to reach out and smooth his hand over where his children grew inside her.

He ignored it.

"Katerina."

Her eyes fluttered open, and for a split second she smiled, but she must have quickly remembered everything, because it died as she straightened and her expression went fully blank. "Ah. We're here," she said flatly.

"Yes, you are home."

Her lips firmed, but she did not argue with him. She allowed him to help her to her feet. They were ushered to the royal car and then driven up the hill to the palace.

Home. With its white walls and spires, tall on the hill that looked down over his island nation. The stars were out tonight, the moon bouncing against the softly crashing surf and the white of the palace, making it glow in the darkness.

Sometimes, late at night like this, he could almost understand why people believed in fairy tales.

Then he remembered his mother's screams.

Katerina said nothing as they drove, which was not unusual exactly. Part of why she'd been such an excellent assistant had been her ability to sit comfortably in silence and stillness without needing to make small talk.

So why it bothered him now, he could not begin to guess. And since he couldn't, he chose to ignore it.

It was the dead of night, and he helped her out of the car at his personal entrance to the castle. He had instructed his staff to take the night off as it was still best to keep everything as under the radar as possible. Only Christos, his driver and head bodyguard, knew about Katerina's return so far.

He wanted to keep it that way for as long as possible. He helped Katerina out of the car and inside. The hallways were lit dimly, as they often were when no one was about, so he took her hand.

"I am sure you are quite hungry. Why don't we go to my private dining room? I will have a meal brought up."

She removed her hand from his and stopped abruptly, turning to face him with raised chin and stubborn brows.

"I think I am too tired. I'm sure you can have a tray sent up to my room, and since I know all the rooms in the palace, you needn't show me where, only tell me."

He opened his mouth to argue, but something about the sharp look in her eyes told him she was *hoping* he would argue. That arguing would fall right into whatever plans she was no doubt already formulating.

Katerina was extraordinarily intelligent and savvy. It was why he'd hired her, and why he'd come to rely on her so.

Still, he would not be so easily maneuvered. He did not argue. He smiled pleasantly. "Why, the queen's bedchamber, of course."

Her mouth dropped open, and this was quite gratifying, if nothing else today had been.

He took her hand once more, and no doubt her shock at his statement kept her from jerking away. He held her gaze as he lifted her hand and brushed his lips across her knuckles.

She let out a shaky breath. Perhaps *two* things were gratifying, because she was not immune to him, and while immunity would be best for both of them, he got a perverse thrill out of her reaction all the same.

"I will have a tray of food sent up at once. I know what you like after all." In concerning detail. He dropped her hand and turned on a heel. If he stayed, he would be tempted.

And it would not do to be tempted.

Just yet. After all, if they were to be married, it would not be quite so necessary to endeavor to keep his hands to himself. They were bound forever now, and why not take the simple pleasures of that when they were pleasurable indeed?

It was too easy to remember that night. The way a simple kiss had turned into a heat that had consumed him. *That* had been a mistake, but it no longer needed to be.

They were to be married.

He had to push those thoughts away as he strode to the kitchens looking for Mrs. Markis, who had been the head of the kitchens since he'd been a boy. He found her already up and serving Zandra in the small dining area that was meant for staff.

"What are you doing up and *here*?" he demanded of his sister.

She raised an eyebrow. "I could ask you the same."

But she shrugged. "I am hungry and I did not wish to wake Lysias. I was going to make myself some tea and a snack, but Mrs. Markis insisted on handling it."

"I did not expect you back this evening, Your Majesty," Mrs. Markis said with a curtsy. "I'll make up a plate for you at once."

"A tray, Mrs. Markis, to take back to my rooms, if you would be so kind. And ensure there are no olives on it, if you would."

She nodded and moved quickly back to the kitchen.

"You love olives," Zandra said, staring at him speculatively.

Diamandis did not justify this comment with a response.

"Where did you disappear to for most of the day, brother?" She smiled at him innocently.

Like she already knew.

He narrowed his eyes. "What do you know?"

"I suppose Lysias heard some whispers that you'd taken a surprise trip to Athens. No one could quite fathom why you would do such a thing." Zandra took a bite of cookie and smiled at him. "Except me, of course."

"Perhaps I simply went to Athens to obtain your wedding present."

She shook her head. "You went to see her, and you went to find the truth. So?"

There was no point wasting time. Zandra had her suspicions and by tomorrow he had to have everything perfectly in place. He would have to work around the clock. "Katerina and I will be married quickly."

"How quickly?"

"As soon as everything is in place. She is very concerned about image and gossip, so we will have to concoct a bit of a story. You're one of the few people who know the truth, Zandra. I'll need you to go along with it."

While his sister was often irreverent, her gaze was serious as she nodded. "What's the story?"

He explained the fake Athens marriage that he would make real. The health issues he would invent. As long as there was a paper trail, no one could prove him wrong.

"Ask Lysias to help you. He's excellent at all those illegal things."

Diamandis scowled. He did not care for *illegal* methods, but he had no doubt Zandra was right. "Very well," he said through gritted teeth, though it added another person who knew the truth. But if there were two people he had learned to trust since he'd taken the crown, it was Zandra and Lysias.

And Katerina.

Zandra finished her cookie and studied him. "You know, if you need to do it quickly… What if you just… took *our* wedding?"

"What do you mean?"

"Lysias and I have no use for some fancy affair—that was *your* insistence. I'm quite happy with the Athenian elopement. So you and Katerina could take our places at the royal wedding. You can say it was the plan all along, and that you were simply waiting for Katerina to be well enough to deal with the responsibilities and attention before you told everyone it was to be *your* wedding. It lends credence."

Diamandis watched Zandra sip her tea as she expressly did not meet his gaze. He wasn't surprised that she did not want the pomp and circumstance of a royal wedding. She had not grown up with it all and was still getting used to the ceremony of being royal.

But what did puzzle him was that she was helping him. "I am surprised you are supporting me in this."

"If I confess that part of why I can't sleep is because of the preparations for this wedding, because my nerves over this grand ceremony keep me awake every night, would you understand better?"

"Is this true? Why didn't you tell me?"

"It would not have changed your mind, and I want to have *some* respect for tradition even though I remember so little. But it has become a larger burden than I anticipated, and I would not be sad at all if you and Katerina took our place." Then her face scrunched up into a frown. "Why would you be surprised at my support?"

He'd walked right into that one. "I am quite tired. I'll go and fetch the tray from Mrs. Markis. Do keep this quiet for the time being until everything is in place."

"Diamandis. She *wants* to marry you, doesn't she?"

He did not look at his sister. "I am sure she came to the same conclusion I did. That this is what's best for everyone involved."

"Anóitos," Zandra said under her breath. "You are not forcing this poor woman to marry you."

"I gave her a choice."

"Oh, I'm sure it was a *great* choice." She muttered a few more choice words for him as she got to her feet and began to pace.

"She is pregnant with my children," Diamandis said, having no idea why he was defending himself when he was king, and he did not need anyone's support.

Everyone had to do what he demanded. "What else am I to do?"

Zandra's hands rose to her own belly bump. "Children...plural?"

Twins. Twins. Twins. He cleared his throat. "Yes. Twins, apparently."

"Like Achilleas and Rafail?"

Diamandis could not confirm this immediately. His throat had grown too tight. Sometimes the things Zandra couldn't remember hit him sideways. Like their brothers.

Sometimes he heard their screams in his sleep, and she did not even remember having met them.

"Yes, like Achilleas and Rafail," he managed roughly.

"I wish..." But she did not voice her wish. She had no need to. He knew she wished she could remember, but sometimes Diamandis felt it was best she did not. She could study the history books, learn the names and faces of her family, but she did not have to live with the bloody reminders of what had happened to them.

She crossed the room and wrapped her arms around him, as if such gestures of affection could ever become commonplace or comfortable. "Take our wedding then." She pulled back and looked up at him. "But maybe don't think of it as royal business and something to be done for the crown, but an opportunity."

"An opportunity for what?"

"For happiness, Diamandis. For love and family."

But Diamandis knew what love did to a family.

It ended it with blood.

Katerina awoke slowly, cuddling deeper into the softness around her. She was half-convinced it was a dream and she'd wake up in her uncomfortable apartment and find that her alarm hadn't gone off that morning.

But she was too warm, too content to worry about that and search for her phone to find out what time it was. She could be late...just this once.

Then there was a...smell. She could not identify it, but she knew. She remembered. She was not in her apartment. She was not living *her* life.

She was a prisoner to the Agonas throne once more. She opened her eyes and stared at the gilt ceiling above her. Because she was in the queen's bedroom, no less.

You will be an effective queen.

Of course she would. As far as she could tell, being the queen was little more than being Diamandis's assistant in public rather than private. She'd been an *excellent* assistant in private, so why would the promotion to public figurehead change that?

Such a promotion. She rolled her eyes here in the privacy of the room where no one would see, then she pushed herself up onto her hands. She was supposed to be more clearheaded today. Ready to problem-solve.

Ready to plan her escape. Again.

But her gaze landed on a tray next to the bed— where she'd left the remains of her dinner last night. At some point when she'd been asleep it had been taken away and replaced with one full of pastries and juices.

She tried very hard not to be happy or excited. It was just *food*, just a *bed*, and the price was her whole life. So she shouldn't enjoy a decadent *bougatsa*, her favorite. She should protest, or something.

But her stomach rumbled, and this had been the best sleep she'd gotten in months. At the end of the day, none of this was ideal, but she was seven months pregnant with twins and someone had made her two meals in a row and she had slept on a bed that felt like being carried away in clouds.

Would it really hurt to enjoy this for a few days while she formulated a plan? She would have to get around Diamandis somehow, but that didn't mean she had to be miserable in the process.

A door opened—she heard it squeak—but the door to the bedroom remained resolutely shut. Which was when she turned her head and saw there was *another* door. A *connecting* door.

As Diamandis strode into her room with no knock, no request to enter, she realized their bedchambers must adjoin.

She scowled deeply. No, she could not stay here and enjoy the amenities for a few days. She needed to find a way out of this now, before she was doomed to spend the rest of her life fending off whispers.

Her mother.

And this pang for a man she would never, ever reach.

"Good morning," Diamandis greeted. He frowned at the tray. "Why haven't you eaten? Is the selection not to your liking? I thought *bougatsa* was your favorite."

Something inside of her fluttered that he might know that. Why would he know that?

It hardly mattered when she had to somehow thwart him and his grand royal plans.

"The selection is just fine. Send my compliments to Mrs. Markis. Or are we still acting secretly? Am I allowed to leave my room?"

"You are the one desperate for secrecy, Katerina," he returned in his stiff manner.

"Only as much as you, Diamandis. Certainly not

more than you want to avoid any reason for someone to suggest you might have disappointed your father."

She did not often stoop to mentioning his parents. He got that cold look on his face that she knew hid pain. So much pain. He did not speak of the *before* times, but it had been clear in her years of working for him that the stories about how devoted the royals were to each other were true, not just fodder to make subjects happy and content that they were led by nice people.

The Agonas family had been a close one, before the coup that had ended most of their lives.

"You have no idea how hard I tried to disappoint my father when he was alive, Katerina. It would be my great pleasure to disappoint him now, if it meant he was here with us. But he is not."

And those words made Katerina feel very, *very* small. As was clearly his intent.

"Everything will be in place by this evening," he said. He stood there, hands behind his back in what she had always called his *proclamation stance*. "We will make an announcement to the press and ask for privacy for a few more days before you are introduced. On Friday. The wedding will be the following week."

Week. *Week.* "Week."

"Yes. It is already settled."

"But it is not. First of all, I have refused to marry you. Second of all, Diamandis, you have no idea what you're getting yourself into marrying a commoner. People accept Lysias marrying your sister because he made himself into a billionaire, because his parents— servants though they might have been—were named martyrs for the Kalyvan cause. I am a bastard commoner. My father's identity is unknown." Sometimes she wasn't even sure her mother knew it. "And my mother… Surely you have looked into my family, Diamandis. If not today, then before you hired me. You have to know that my blood will never be considered fit for royalty."

He stood there and his face betrayed nothing. "I do not wish to speak ill of your mother. It is of no matter."

Of no matter? Katerina did not know how any living man could be so stubborn. She got out of bed, unable to sit still while he stood above her like some kind of…

Well, king.

She was shorter than him, so he was still looking down at her, but at least she felt like she had an almost equally powerful position by standing up to him.

The bed was safely between them. She needed that safety or she might—

No, she could not give in to him again, not when she had so much to lose. She could not let this flutter turn into the twirling, desperate hold of need.

She had learned her lesson. She could not forget it.

"Then allow me to speak ill of her for you because it *does* matter. She is a gold digger. A narcissist. And I have been as far beneath her notice as possible since I flat-out refused to sneak her into any of your events so she could mix and mingle with what few men of power she hasn't yet slept with or attempted to."

"I do not see what this has to do with you."

"How can you *not* see? You are a king."

"Yes," he agreed, taking a few steps toward the end of the bed. "And as king, it is quite easy for me to keep your mother as far out of your life as you wish."

What might her life have been if *anyone* had been

able to keep Ghavriella Floros as far away from her life as she wished.

But Katerina could not change the past. Or who her mother was. She could only focus on extricating herself from this mess before it was announced. Before she was married.

Before you give in. Again.

"If you had gone to your council before any of this had happened and proposed me as your future queen, not one of them would have given you their support."

He lifted a shoulder as he came around to her side of the bed. She was now trapped, between bed and wall. "I would never seek the council's approval for my future wife. *I* am the one who has to live with her." His gaze moved over her then, and she saw all the things she should ignore. Should fight.

Interest.

Desire.

Need.

She did not understand how, when she felt as unwieldly as an elephant, this kind of heat could bloom within her. How she could burn at all for a man— let alone *this* man, who infuriated her beyond reason. Whom she had run from, because he could be far too cold when he wanted to be.

But she could imagine it all too clearly. His hands, his mouth. The way he had made her feel that night—as though she was lit up from within. How she had shattered, beautifully. There had been no coldness then. Only heat. Only them.

She could not fall for this again. It was a lie. A trick. A temptation meant to ruin them both, maybe. And she didn't wish that for either of them. She couldn't risk it for her children.

You are already pregnant. What more harm can be done?

She blinked at that unbidden thought. And when she lifted her gaze from Diamandis's mouth to his eyes, she felt as though he'd read her thoughts. Down to that one.

It was as though they were tied by that thought, brought increasingly closer against their wills. Some magnetic pull that would ruin them both.

And she struggled to care. Just like that night.

"Katerina," he said, and she must have misheard the gravel in his voice because he kept talking about his plans. "The plans are in motion. You will be my wife and Kalyva's queen." He moved forward and took her hands in his. "Trust me. I will take care of all your many concerns."

She hated that she did trust him. That for all these years she had gotten to know the man under the armor and had come to care for that man. But how she felt didn't matter. It couldn't. Not when she had two children to consider.

"The royal doctor will check you out today to make certain you are healthy and well enough to deal with crowds and wedding preparations. We will not do anything to risk your health or the children's. I am led to understand that twin pregnancies can be difficult."

"My doctor also cautioned me in regard to that, but so far I have had a very routine pregnancy," she said, knowing she should pull her hands away. Knowing she should put more distance between them.

But he was closer somehow. Toe to toe, his head bent toward hers so that when he spoke, his breath danced across her cheek. She wanted to lean. She wanted to forget everything—this was his power, and no matter how she knew he would use it against her, no matter how strong she was, *this* was the thing she could not best, could not escape, could not survive.

"This is excellent news."

"Why?" she asked breathlessly. Stupidly. What was she doing here? Surely he wasn't going to—

But his mouth crashed to hers, exactly as it had done that night—fierce, cunning, and confident that she would not resist.

Because she could not. She was powerless in the face of him, in the face of the heat that erupted between them when they got too close. Even knowing it was wrong and she would regret it, her body simply insisted she give in, as if it cared not at all what her mind told it.

So she did. She gave in, held on, kissed him back with all the passion that had not died inside of her though she had tried desperately to quash it—both before and after.

She fell into the maddening heat all over again. No matter the many costs.

CHAPTER FIVE

LUST WAS LIKE some kind of wildfire in Diamandis's mind, turning every rational, important thought to ash. When Katerina had been his assistant, when he'd felt such a loss of control coming over him, he'd been able to order her away, to excuse himself.

Except that one time. When it hadn't been work, but…disaster.

That one time, which had haunted him every night since. He'd controlled himself because there was only ruin if he didn't. Because she knew too much…and those who knew that much had only betrayed him.

When he'd come into her room this morning, he'd tried to remind himself of the inevitable betrayal, the inevitable end and loss—all the ways he could not trust what he felt, because the crown came first. All the ways she should never trust him because, deep down, he was not what he seemed.

But she'd been sitting in the bed, hair rumpled, cheeks flushed from the warmth of the blankets and pillows piled around her. He'd seen the swell of her belly where their children grew and it had given new fangs to old feelings he thought he'd vanquished.

Then she'd gotten out of bed, wearing an oversize

T-shirt that barely skimmed her thighs and was most certainly not fit for the queen she would soon be. Her feet were bare, her hair a sleep-tangled maze of curls. He had never seen her in such a state.

He'd tried, valiantly—if he did say so himself—to resist. But she was like a magnet. She was like air, and he had forgotten how to breathe.

There was no choice but to kiss her. No choice but to devour her mouth as he once had. But this time his hands moved over her round belly, marveling at what he had had a hand in creating.

She was carrying his children. She would be his wife—no matter how many objections she tried to throw at him. The plans were in motion; *everything* was in motion. It was a risk to form this union, but letting her go would be a bigger one.

So why shouldn't this be his reward?

Particularly when she met his kiss with all the passion she had shown him that night, as though she too had been fighting to hold herself back from this.

This. A need like no other. And for those first few weeks after, he'd been able to convince himself that he had solved the problem by giving in that night. That by tasting her, by being inside her, he knew what it was and could then resist it. A known enemy was always better than a mysterious threat.

But he knew, here in this moment of heat and passion and desire, that it had not been his impressive control or some vanquished feeling that had kept him from kissing her again.

It had been *fear* that had meant he'd kept his hands to himself in those weeks afterward. Fear that nothing else could ever match *this*, and it was best never to know it again. Fear that she'd seen too much, and now held too much power over him. She might be a good person, but he was not, and if he fell into forgetting that, too much was at stake.

But Katerina was inextricably linked to him now. There was no turning back or sending her away. He would have to find a way to win when she was in his orbit because she would be Kalyva's queen. *His* queen.

Something strange roared inside of him—too many emotions that if he named would become unwieldy. Dangerous.

So he pushed his thoughts away and focused on the taste of her. The way she moaned as his hands slid under the ridiculous T-shirt she wore, to find warm skin, soft and supple. Her rounded belly, her delectable breasts, nipples pebbled tight and wanting just for him.

"Diamandis."

His name on her lips, her breathless sighs, and the way she gave in to him after spending so much time fighting with him... She was a curse, and he reveled in it.

He pulled the T-shirt off her, revealing her beautiful body. She fumbled with the buttons of his shirt as his fingers dove into her tangled hair. As he drowned in the pleasure of her mouth once more. As she rid him of his shirt, her own hands touring his body as though he were her long-lost lover, returned from the unknown. As if she were desperate for someone she'd once lost.

But he had not been lost. She'd *left*.

That might have broken through the thick sexual haze, maybe, but she ripped her mouth from his.

"Diamandis. This... We... I'm too...big." But this was not a refusal. Not a *no*. It was merely...foolish self-doubt, when she was nothing short of perfect. She was the only woman who had ever tested him, ever bested him.

"You are a goddess," he murmured, lowering himself from her mouth to the round glory of her breasts, her stomach, and lower still.

She sank onto the bed and he got to his knees to worship her, spreading her out on the bed behind them, drinking deep until she was shaking and saying his name, over and over in breathless desire.

But he wanted more than his name. More than her hands in his hair and the taste of her a drug he'd never survive. He had had her once and had convinced himself it was enough.

But he hadn't looked twice at another woman since and had not allowed himself to ask why that might be. Why she was not interchangeable with any other woman who might share his bed. Why he missed her voice crisply correcting him on something or another.

Or moaning out his name.

He stood and she looked up at him, flushed and dazed and so wholly perfect in every way. "But… how…"

He did not care *how*, only that he was inside her. He got onto the bed with her, then maneuvered her on top of him, naked and wanton, while he still wore his pants, though she'd disposed of his shirt.

She fumbled with the button on his slacks but did not make it to the zipper because he needed something from her first. He did not seek to understand why. He just wanted it, so he would demand it.

He was the king.

The whys did not matter.

He clamped his hands over her wrists before she could succeed in unzipping his pants. "Say it."

Misty green eyes met his. "Say what?" she returned, breathless and flushed.

"You know what I want to hear, Katerina."

She swallowed. She was straddling him, needy for him, and yet there was hesitation in her eyes. Not over the act, no. She wanted him as desperately as he wanted her. And he was so lost he might capitulate without getting what he desired.

Impossible.

"Please," she said, so quietly he almost didn't hear it. "My king."

He freed himself from his pants, not waiting for her to do it. Not waiting for her to sheath herself on him. The position, the place did not matter—the need was the same and all-encompassing. He took control and moved inside her, enjoying the exquisite, inexorable fit.

She was his perfection. She was meant for this and for him. He could not give her or himself everything, but he would give them this.

His hands slid up her thighs, to rest at her hips. He guided her in the rhythm he wanted, needed. Her head fell back as she lost herself in the pleasure of their bodies meeting.

She sobbed his name as she shattered around him, over and over again, her hair tumbling around her shoulders, her skin flushed with exertion and pleasure. She was art, and everything centered on her. Even as his blood roared in his ears, as the spiking flame of need threatened to explode, he waited. He moved, he absorbed, and he *waited* for that one thing he desired.

"My king," she rasped once more, sending him over the edge with her.

Katerina did not know what had come over her, but this was not a new feeling. She'd felt the same that night months ago, in the aftermath of reckless pleasure—she did not know who that woman was. It was a stranger who'd taken over her body, who had enjoyed a man she knew would never give her what she wanted.

She should hate that stranger who was so weak, but she felt too good. Warm and sated. Comfortable and content. A future did not matter in the present of satisfied need. Oh, this was very bad. Because Diamandis no doubt saw this as a win, but...

Well, she'd won too. If only temporarily.

She turned her head to look at him, expecting to see the same sort of reaction she'd seen on him in his office—a slow, dawning horror at his loss of control, a stiff, detached mask as he withdrew, which made it very clear what a mistake they'd made.

But he did not look stiff in the here and now. He did not move to straighten his clothes or make a careful, dignified retreat.

He lounged there in her bed, looking quite content, arms thrown back behind his head, showcasing all that muscle she'd just enjoyed. But it wasn't the sleek lines, the rangy body, the way every masculine part of him made her heart beat triple-time. It was the expression on his face.

She could not call anything about Diamandis soft,

but there was a relaxed air to him that went deeper than just sexual satisfaction. He looked...content.

Her heart ached. When had she ever seen him enjoy any sliver of contentment? It was very rare. She could count the times on one hand, and those moments never lasted more than a few seconds because he felt he was under constant scrutiny, and any hint at enjoyment sent the *wrong* message.

She still remembered the first time he'd truly smiled in her presence. She had been frustrated with another one of his diatribes on tradition and propriety. She had picked up a dark, shriveled pebble from the grounds and handed it to him.

Here. I think you lost your soul.

He had looked at the rock, and then his mouth had curved. For a moment, true humor had danced there.

This was the problem with Diamandis. Even as he was taking over her life, threatening everything she wanted for her children, she found herself incapable of ruining this moment. She was glad he seemed content. A joke about his black soul was one of the few things that had ever made him laugh in her presence. It was clear that reality and Diamandis's many responsibilities and duties would crash down upon them soon enough.

"I have much to do," he said, his voice a shade rough, his tone more philosophical than determined to make any movement or action.

"Then you should do it," Katerina said agreeably.

But they both lay there, maybe an inch of space between them, not touching.

This was her fate. She saw it so starkly. She could have pieces of him and she could control certain aspects of him, but there would always be this invisible line between them. And if it was between him and her, it would exist between him and their children as well.

Could she bear it? Could she ask her as of yet unborn children to bear it too?

"You may choose your own staff as you see fit once the announcement is made," he said, switching to business so easily she hated that she'd given him an ounce of contentment. "I trust you know everyone currently on staff except your replacement. You may choose from the current pool, or I can bring in applicants as you wish."

"I'm sure the current pool is sufficient, though I would be very interested in meeting my replacement." She watched him then, wondering whether he would ever look at her, or would simply stare at the gilt ceiling until he rolled off the bed, tucked himself away, and left her alone.

"He is…not as good as you," Diamandis said carefully, "But then, you left very big shoes to fill."

It was a compliment that should not make her happy, and yet it did. She had taken pride in her work, in making herself indispensable. *In proving your mother wrong.*

Ugh.

She pulled the blanket tightly around her. The thought of her mother was a stark reminder that she was, at her core, not any better. She was a slave to her wants and damn the consequences.

She heard a rustle of movement, felt the mattress dip then pop back. Diamandis was getting up. He was leaving.

And what the hell was she supposed to do now? Run? Try to convince him, yet again, that marriage wasn't possible and that he should let her go? She knew how it worked, even if not how this specific thing worked. The wheels of his plans were already in motion, and nothing would stop them.

"I think we should put off any announcements, Diamandis," she said, sounding stronger than she felt. "I am not convinced this is the correct course of action."

He shrugged. "I am."

He spoke as if that was it. As if that was all that mattered.

Oh, how she wished she had the energy to punch him. "I know what it is to grow up in a house devoid of love and warmth, Diamandis. I may not have grown up in the castle, but I had quite a few luxuries. It did not make up for my mother's cruelty."

"There is a big space between love and cruelty, Katerina. I will not be cruel to you or our children. I will never love anyone, but that does not mean we cannot share a mutual sort of respect for one another."

It hurt. Far more than it should considering she knew this man, maybe better than he knew himself. "Is that what we're calling it?" she returned, incapable of keeping the acid out of her tone.

His mouth firmed. "It does not have to be a mistake, Katerina. It could simply be life. Is it really so much worse than scratching by, alone and destitute in a hovel in Athens?"

"You're such a snob, Diamandis. Just because it wasn't a castle doesn't mean I was destitute."

"I may not have experienced it myself, but I am well acquainted with what poverty looks like, and how hard people have to work to survive it. I cannot understand why you'd choose to struggle like that when you could have this." He waved his hand as if to encompass the palace.

And the thing was, she didn't fully understand it, either. Which sacrifice was better for her children? She couldn't seem to come to a conclusion that settled her. No conclusion was the right one. No choice gave them everything.

"Zandra didn't go running back to the streets of Athens just because she didn't like some elements of royalty."

"I am not your sister. You cannot *save* me from a life I have chosen with my own free will." *I would choose you*, she realized. And it hurt, because she knew he would never choose her.

Only Kalyva.

And yet, he was not *totally* wrong, was he? If they could somehow avoid the whispers that had tormented her in her childhood, then this would be quite the life for her children. The best of everything. Was her pride more important than that?

She didn't know. She just didn't know.

But Diamandis certainly thought he did. "We shall see." And then he left.

Without looking back.

CHAPTER SIX

DIAMANDIS SPENT THE remainder of the morning hard at work. There was much to do and he'd spent over an hour.. not working.

He was going through with the announcement. And if there was a strange tug of discomfort deep in his gut, he ignored it. Because there was nothing to be guilty about. He was doing what was right.

No, he could not promise Katerina some fairy-tale love and warmth. He knew all too well where that led, and he would protect his children. Loving them would only leave him open to the sorts of things that had been his father's downfall. His most trusted adviser had made this clear to Diamandis on the very day of his parents' deaths: that if his father had not been blinded by love, he would have seen through the cracks in the kingdom. He would have been able to stop the coup before it had started.

Love was a death sentence.

But he could promise Katerina everything else she could possibly want, and he firmly believed in what he'd said to her this morning. There was space between love and cruelty, where his secrets could remain in the dark—where they belonged. It was a space where love did not threaten everything. He could exist in the middle. And would, as he had all these years.

He entered the dining room a few minutes later than usual and frowned when only Lysias and Zandra were present. "Where is Katerina?"

Zandra's eyebrows rose. "Are we supposed to know? I thought you had her locked up in a dungeon so no one would know she was here."

"My assistant was supposed to notify you both of today's change of plans. We have put the announcement in motion. After dinner, the four of us will address the council and explain the change in wedding participants."

His sister and brother-in-law exchanged glances. "I haven't seen Tomás today," Zandra finally said, somewhat reluctantly. "But perhaps he left word and it didn't make it to us."

Diamandis's temper flared. He'd gone through three assistants since Katerina had left, each more useless than the last. "I wish I could continue to give him the benefit of the doubt."

"Well, he's afraid of you, Diamandis. Hard to blame him for that."

"So hiding from me and not doing his work will fix the problem?"

"He's young," Zandra said, but it was clear she was enjoying defending Tomás, not because she thought he warranted defending, but because she liked to frustrate her older brother.

"He's useless. Messages never went astray when Katerina was my assistant," Diamandis muttered, wondering how long he would last before he went and hunted her down himself.

"Should I point out that Ms. Floros is no longer his assistant, or would you like to?" Lysias said to his wife.

Diamandis scowled at them both, but he did not have a rejoinder because the door was opened and Katerina stepped inside.

She curtsied, and he knew the symbol of deference was more habit than actual deference, at least toward him. "Your Majesty. Your Highness. Mr. Balaskas. Or have you conferred a title on your brother-in-law as I suggested many months ago?" She smiled sweetly up at him.

The smile was exactly the one she used to bestow upon him regularly, once upon a time, when she'd been his assistant, suggesting things she thought he should have already done. He did not understand what twisted inside of him, only that he wished they were alone so he did not have to keep his hands to himself.

She was dressed for dinner in a plain black dress that hugged the glorious swell of her bump. He had to force himself to look away so he did not picture what it might look like if he peeled the dress away.

"You are late."

"I did not know I was allowed to leave my prison until just recently. Luckily a maid was available to help me dress as I also discovered that my bag with all my things in it had been confiscated."

"It is best if you look fit to be queen when around the palace. Your old clothes were *not* that."

"Perhaps we should leave you two to quarrel over dinner without us?" Zandra suggested, her glass hiding her face—though Diamandis had no doubt she was hiding a smile behind it.

"That will not be necessary," Diamandis replied

stiffly. He moved to the chair next to him and pulled it out for Katerina before the waiting staff member could.

Katerina hesitated, though he couldn't imagine why. But she sat without saying anything. Diamandis took his own seat, royal protocol not necessary at a family meal.

Family. After years of it just being Diamandis, the past few months had been an adjustment. There was his sister, and Lysias, who had once been as close as a brother to him before...

Everything had been destroyed that night, and he had never thought there would be any recourse. But Zandra and Lysias...

And now Katerina. Who was to be his wife. The mother of his children. Family, in all those ways he'd promised he'd never have.

But life changed on you, this he knew quite intimately. He was rolling with the punches, as one must. As a king must.

"How are you feeling, Katerina?" Zandra asked as the staff began to serve dinner.

"Well enough. I am very fortunate that I've had such an uneventful pregnancy. Twins can often be complicated."

"It's hard to imagine that soon enough we will have *three* children running about the palace." Zandra smiled broadly. "I don't remember much of my childhood here, but I remember the feeling of being glad I had so many other children to play with, even if I was much younger. I can't wait for..."

Diamandis tuned her out. Because *he* remembered. In color. He could hear his brothers' voices even now.

They had loved to play pranks on him—the angrier he got, the more hilarious they had found it.

Their laughter haunted his dreams. As did every cruel word he'd ever uttered to them, thinking himself better—older, more mature, the *heir*. A person with real responsibilities, while they got to *play*.

He could remember Zandra as a little girl. Their mother had given her too much freedom, in Diamandis's estimation. The girl had always followed him about, and when he'd return her to the children's wing or tell her that he was busy with important things, she would poke him in the throat.

Hard.

He remembered, too well, taking all of them for granted. Their love, their existence. He assumed Zandra could only bear it because she remembered so little.

And none of the aftermath.

Wasn't she lucky?

"Diamandis?"

It was Katerina, looking at him like he'd never wanted her to: with a sympathetic kind of understanding, when there was nothing to understand.

Everyone but Zandra had been murdered. The end.

"We will approach the committee as a unit," he said, not worried about whatever conversation they'd been having that he hadn't been paying attention to. They were eating together to discuss business. "They will no doubt have some questions and concerns, but we will assuage them all." He gestured to Lysias. "Thanks to Lysias, we already have an Athenian marriage certificate, dated late last year."

"I assure you, no one would ever question the validity," Lysias said, smiling broadly at Katerina. "It's amazing what money can buy."

Diamandis endeavored to keep the conversation to subjects like the council and what would happen next, but Zandra somehow kept bringing up children and families. Diamandis forced himself to eat, though everything tasted like ash in his mouth.

He would not think about these things. He would no longer engage in these dinners. This was about the crown, not *family*.

When he was certain Katerina and Zandra had eaten their fill, he signaled the staff to begin taking things away.

"Is everyone finished? We must head down to the throne room. The council should be assembling as we speak." He did not look at Katerina as he offered her his arm.

This wasn't about her, or about their children, or about his sister, and most of all not about his childhood.

It was about the throne. It was about lines of succession and making sure nothing tarnished what his father had left him any more than he already had.

When Diamandis held out his hand for her, Katerina only hesitated for a moment before she took it.

It was now or never. If she went along with him to this council meeting, it was all over.

Are you really going through with this?

He led her into the hallway and toward the throne room without question, without hesitation. In his mind, it was already done. That alone should make her balk.

She watched him as he kept his gaze straight ahead, jaw clenched tight as it often was before he faced the council.

She knew she did not have to be by his side—as future queen or former assistant. *She* had the choice here, but...

Her choice had already been made when she came to dinner. It had been the doctor's visit earlier that had swayed her. Not the royal doctor she'd expected, whom she'd always found a bit aloof, but a woman, maybe in her forties, who had brought along a specialist who was well acquainted with multiple births and high-risk pregnancies.

They had gone over not just where she was at now—heartbeats and everything healthy and as they should be—but what was still to come. How they would care for her and her babies in labor and delivery and address any complications that could come up.

Katerina would never be able to afford such care on her own, and the risks with twins were higher. By leaving the palace, by refusing to be Diamandis's queen, she was risking *all* of their lives.

Or perhaps you really just want to be his queen.

She closed her eyes as Diamandis led her up the aisle of the grand ballroom. The council liked to have their meetings here and hear their voices bounce loudly against the high vaulted ceilings back to their own ears. They liked to look up at the king on his gold, jeweled throne and fancy themselves important for serving him.

Katerina had always thought it a foolish exercise

in grandiose wealth and self-importance, and now she was being led up to sit on a throne. The queen's throne.

Instead of standing in the shadows as she'd once done.

There was no turning back if she did this. No escaping. Once their marriage was announced to the council, it was over.

She'd gone to dinner. She hadn't attempted to talk Diamandis out of his plan. Part of her understood how stupid this was, and yet...

She could not turn her back on all that the kingdom would offer her children, and so she had made her decision. The doctor had warmly informed her that everything was good and she would be by her side through the remainder of the pregnancy as well as after, and so Katerina had decided that she would do this. For the opportunities it would give her children.

Diamandis might not love them, but *she* would be all the love their children needed. She would shield them from every rumor, every whisper. She was not her mother and so she would put her children above herself.

Always.

And none of those decisions revolved around Diamandis. Not really. She couldn't control him. She couldn't change his mind or make him want to be a loving father.

She watched him as he took his seat on the king's throne and gestured for her to take the queen's.

She would never reach him. But that did not mean she could not make something positive out of this... strange situation. Make *many* positives. Just as she had when she was his assistant.

She could live without his love. She'd lived without her mother's. She'd survived and somehow managed to be a rather decent human being, she liked to think.

So she sat. In the queen's chair. In *her* chair. She could apply herself to being queen and mother just as she had to being an essential assistant.

That will not make him love you.

She frowned at the insidious thought, and luckily she had no time to really think it over as the council approached and took their seats at the table situated in front of the thrones.

Lysias joined them at the table as though he was now a member of the council—and this was new, as were a few of the faces. This was, after all, not the first council meeting to which Katerina had been privy. While there were often parts of the meeting she and other staff were asked to withdraw from so delicate conversations could be had in private and away from the untrustworthy help, she had been Diamandis's right hand man in many meetings.

She didn't like them. She found most of the men on Diamandis's council far too stuffy, traditional and cruel. More often than not, she left said meetings complaining to Diamandis and urging him to consider a council purge.

He had refused, of course. It had taken Lysias producing evidence proving that a few of the members had been planning to betray Diamandis all those months ago to bring in these new faces.

Katerina had her doubts that this new group would be any better, considering two of the men she'd long hated the most were still on it. But Diamandis must have listened to her at least a little, because some of the new faces were younger. Two were even women.

"Council members, thank you for agreeing to meet on such short notice," Diamandis said. "We have come in front of you this evening to announce a few changes to the royal wedding."

One of the men she didn't like—who was closest to Diamandis, much to her eternal consternation—Marias Remis, turned to Lysias. "Did this really necessitate a meeting?"

Lysias did not respond. He merely pointed to Diamandis.

"It will not be Princess Zandra and Mr. Balaskas's wedding next week. I know that is what we had led you to believe, but this was a ruse to keep my wife safe and healthy."

"Your…?"

Murmurs amongst the council members sounded like a dull buzz to Katerina, and it reminded her of how often she had been the reason for the buzz of gossip—or rather, her mother had been the reason. Katerina had dealt with the fallout.

"Some of you will remember Ms. Floros," Diamandis continued over the buzz that had Katerina curling her hands around the arms of the chair to keep herself from running out of the ballroom. "Unfortunately, she has been plagued by some ill health. This is why she stepped down as my assistant. Though we wanted to marry, we knew Katerina was not strong enough yet to withstand the rigors of a royal wedding and all that goes with it, so we were married in Athens."

"Athens!" someone said, as if Diamandis had claimed they'd been married on Mars.

"This is incredibly unorthodox, Your Majesty," Marias said disapprovingly.

"It is, and I think you all know how much I regret any behavior that could be so described. However, Katerina's health made keeping this under wraps incredibly important. I could hardly ask her to carry the weight of the kingdom when she was in such a state. But she is much improved, and the doctors have assured us that the pregnancy is coming along quite well. We wanted to ensure, Katerina's health withstanding, that we could have an official, traditional wedding before the twins are born."

There was a moment of quiet, short-lived. Marias stood and spoke as if he was speaking for everyone.

"Your Majesty, this is impossible. And seems incredibly far-fetched."

Diamandis stood abruptly, and the whole table not only quieted but stilled. Even the pompous Marias did not dare speak when Diamandis looked down at him in clear censure.

"Regardless of how it might seem to you, this is the truth, and I would think long and hard before you question it again."

Marias bowed his head. "Yes, Your Majesty."

Diamandis sat once more. "We knew we wouldn't be able to plan it quickly enough, so we began preparations with the ruse of using the princess and her husband as the bride and groom. Surely you can understand that our subterfuge was necessary in order to protect Katerina's health."

He sounded so…calculated, Katerina thought. And she knew that was what the council required. It was how he always spoke to them. They always had more arguments when Diamandis showed any emotions—usually frustration.

He knew how to play them, and she knew that they did not like this. It wasn't just the open questions, the little comments about *unorthodox* and *tradition* and *your parents*. It was the way they looked at her.

Like she was gum to be scraped off Diamandis's shoe. She raised her chin in response. She had spent her whole life fielding looks like that.

And you wanted to escape them, remember?

It was an impossible choice. The best doctors, the best chance for health and survival versus the way these men looked at her and how they would likely look at her children.

But her children would have *love*. If not their father's, then their mother's.

And Katerina would make certain that was all that mattered.

CHAPTER SEVEN

THE MEETING WAS INTERMINABLE. The questions, the pearl-clutching so over the top that Diamandis's head throbbed with poorly leashed anger.

He had not expected his council, aside from Lysias, to take all of this information well, but he hadn't anticipated that so many of his council members would make so little attempt to veil their distaste for a *commoner*—something many of them were themselves, having only risen in rank by their wealth and position on this council.

Katerina had warned him, and he had not listened. It would not be the first time. She had a better sense of people than he did—a fact that had always irked.

And now, it will make her an excellent queen.

He let that thought be a kind of balm. Perhaps he had not chosen this. Perhaps his plan had been to never wed and instead to pass along the throne to Zandra or her children. This would have been a decent enough plan.

But having an effective queen to act as his partner, rather than simply waiting to die, was perhaps a better option. Perhaps.

"I am not sure how the people will react to this, Your Majesty," Marias said. Again.

Next to him, Katerina sighed. Loudly. Diamandis gave her a censuring look, but she did not temper her response. Instead, she leaned forward.

"May I address the council?"

Diamandis was surprised by the request but nodded. This was an interesting turn of events. Though she had been present at many a council meeting before, she'd never spoken at one.

She got to her feet and surveyed the table of people below. "Marias," she said, when she probably should have called him "Mr. Remis." "It is interesting to me that you are suddenly worried about what the people will think, when I've heard you, more than once, insist that the throne is more important than the opinion of its subjects."

"This is *about* the throne," Marias returned. "And who should sit upon it."

"And why should I not, Marias? What's done is done. Diamandis and I are married—regardless of Kalyvan ceremony. As you can see, I am quite pregnant. With twins. What would the people think, on the other hand, if Diamandis discarded me and my children?"

Marias puffed out his chest. "That is hardly what I'm suggesting."

"Then what *are* you suggesting?" she returned, as though she genuinely wanted to hear an answer to that. As though she was waiting with bated breath for him to explain himself.

She was beautiful. Diamandis had never considered what it might be like to have a partner in this. Zandra had slowly begun to take on some responsibilities as a working royal, but she didn't yet feel comfortable dealing with the politics of things, though she was studying hard to prepare herself. She was just so behind, so out of step, after having lived twenty years on her own and having little to no memory of Kalyva.

But Katerina didn't need to study. As his former assistant she was abreast of everything, except maybe what little had changed in the past few months. She had always been keen, savvy, and clearheaded.

She had always been an effective tool to utilize... and now she would be more than that. She would be a partner.

Could his biggest mistake actually work out in his favor? It was hard to imagine. But Marias was standing there, open-mouthed, as if desperate to say something but incapable of coming up with the words.

Diamandis stood. "Katerina is right. What's done is done. This was not a meeting to open the floor to opposition. It was a meeting to inform you of what has already taken place and of what will be taking place shortly. If you cannot agree, then I will gladly take letters of resignation."

Marias sat, unmoving. No one else said anything. Satisfied, Diamandis held out his hand to Katerina and led her out of the room, followed by Lysias and Zandra.

"Bravo, Katerina," Zandra said, coming forward to link her arm with Katerina's free one. "Honestly, why do we have this ridiculous committee?"

"Are you calling me ridiculous?" Lysias asked his wife, teasingly.

"The council is tradition," Diamandis said firmly before Zandra and Lysias bantered more—a situation that always reminded him of his parents. "Besides, a king making proclamations without listening to anyone else is a dangerous precedent to set. They will all have roles to play in the ceremony now that it is my wedding instead of yours."

He stopped. "Tomorrow will be a long day as we work on changing the wedding preparations. Katerina, I will walk you back to your rooms. Lysias, Zandra, I bid you good night." He gave them a quick nod, then led Katerina away and toward the king and queen's quarters.

He opened the door that led into her sitting room for her. He followed her inside, not sure what his purpose was.

Are you not?

She played with the bracelet she wore, crossing to the big glass door that would take her outside to the balcony. She did not go out, just looked at the night outside.

"You were magnificent," Diamandis said, standing behind her, admiring what the moonlight did to her olive skin.

"I was tired. I should have handled it more diplomatically. That's why I was a better assistant than speaker."

"It was just what was needed. A strong queen is a good symbol for our people." He reached out and stroked his finger down the elegant curve of her neck.

But she stiffened, turning to face him and holding out a hand as if to ward him off. He looked down at it, then raised an eyebrow at her. Her green eyes were direct, everything about her...cool.

"I have come to a decision," she said very firmly.

"Oh?" he returned.

"You have made your position quite clear. Respect but not love, and I can live with this."

Her words confused him because he thought that had long since been decided. "Wonderful."

"However, you will no: share my bed, nor I yours. We will go back to the way our relationship was—but with more equality, of course. We will be business partners—in the ruling of Kalyva, in the raising of our children—but we will not blur the lines with anything else."

He kept himself very still and did not let the response clawing within him take root. She could make whatever decisions she wished. He was not the kind of man who forced a woman to do his bidding.

But that didn't mean he had to *like* what decision she'd come to. Or how it would prove...difficult. "I suppose you expect me to find my pleasures elsewhere?" he returned coldly.

She blinked. Clearly she had not thought of *that*. He took some grim satisfaction in the frown that caused a crease to form on her forehead.

"I do not think that kind of behavior would befit a king," she said stiffly. Stiff was usually *his* reaction.

"On the contrary. It has been the kind of behavior that has befitted many a king. Not my father, of course, but he loved his wife and she him." Their love had caused a softness, indeed the very blind spot that had ended too many lives.

Something passed over her face then, a kind of shuttering in her eyes that he had seen before but had never understood. And he didn't understand it now, but he felt something twist inside of him in response all the same. *Guilt*, a voice whispered, but he pushed it away. Especially since the voice sounded like his long-dead mother.

"If it is not for love, then we should go about it as business," she said firmly. "If you need to seek pleasures elsewhere… I suppose that is your business. But it won't be mine."

There was nothing to say to that. Nothing to do about it. She was probably right. This was best. A business partnership, nothing more. Just as he'd always wanted.

He left her, knowing he had won a victory, but the expected satisfaction didn't follow. Because no matter what he knew to be the case, it felt like she had come out on top.

Katerina did not sleep well. She wished she could lay the blame on pregnancy, or even on Diamandis himself, but it was her own weakness. If she were stronger, she wouldn't have given in to him.

Twice.

If she hadn't been at his mercy, if she hadn't felt all they could create between them, it wouldn't feel like such a mistake to resist him now.

The thought of him with another woman made her want to retch. She was trying to be philosophical about it. Mature and worldly. Because this was *not* a romantic marriage. It was a protective one. A *business* one.

So he could do…whatever he wanted. With whomever he wanted. She would not be her mother throwing very public fits when half the time *she* had been the other woman. Like with the principal when Katerina was thirteen.

And the fit had been in the middle of her lunch hour at school.

Well, you won't be doing that. So.

So. Maybe she would be uncomfortable. Maybe she would hate it, and maybe she would even feel like throwing a very public fit.

But she wouldn't. Because her life wasn't about Diamandis. It was about her children. It would always be about her children.

She told herself this, over and over again, as she got ready for breakfast. She would be meeting with some of the staff after the meal to determine who might be her own assistant. She had two people in mind with whom she'd worked, though it was still hard to fathom relinquishing control of her life to an assistant when doing the work had always been her job.

Maybe, once she'd had the babies and recovered, she could phase out having an assistant. But for now, she needed help. Especially with the royal wedding next week.

She didn't mind the idea of the spectacle. She was used to hiding in the shadows, so being in the spotlight would be new, but she'd spent the past few years watching how Diamandis handled it, and she'd often had to instruct rooms full of people how to behave according to royal protocol. She wasn't afraid of crowds or attention.

But once it was announced, once the wedding had happened, not only would her every move be scrutinized, but so would Diamandis's.

What would be whispered about her when he was seen gallivanting about with other women?

Maybe she didn't want breakfast after all. Maybe a walk would be better. But just as she was about to pass the dining room entrance and head toward the back of the castle where she could take a walk, she heard Zandra call her name.

Katerina turned to see Zandra a ways behind her. Katerina stopped and Zandra met her at the dining room entrance.

"Are you coming to eat?" Zandra asked pleasantly.

Katerina thought about denying it, but instead she smiled. "Yes."

"Excellent. I cannot eat enough to satisfy this child." She patted her little belly bump. "So I eat an early breakfast by myself, then a second breakfast with Lysias and Diamandis once they're done with their manly grunting."

"Lysias joins Diamandis for his workouts?" Katerina asked with some surprise as they walked into the dining room and took seats at a table already set with platters of food. Just a few months ago, Diamandis had insisted his morning physical activity be a completely solitary endeavor. Even his guards were only allowed to stand outside or watch from afar.

He had been quite adamant about it.

"Yes, it's become quite the thing. Oh, Diamandis was a bit stuffy about it at first, but I'm determined to see them friends again. Did you know that? That they were boyhood friends?"

Katerina smiled as Zandra began to fill two plates without even asking what Katerina wanted. It was the kind of familiar gesture for which their relationship didn't really have any foundation, but Katerina appreciated Zandra for just accepting her and treating her like part of the family, with no questions or concerns.

No snooty words, like the council last night.

"I did know that," Katerina returned, deciding to

pour tea for both of them while Zandra handled the food. "Or surmised it, I suppose. Diamandis never came out and said it directly."

"No, he doesn't do that much, does he?"

Katerina felt the familiar twist of empathy for the man. No matter how angry she was, no matter how determined she was to forge a business partnership with him rather than any kind of friendship or romance, he brought out a reaction in her that drew her back to him.

"It is...very hard to read him at times," Katerina said carefully. It was an odd line to tightrope. She did not wish to speak ill of him to anyone, nor did she want to say something that might offend Zandra, but part of her hoped for a friend with whom she could be honest.

Zandra nodded, taking a bite of her breakfast sausage and chewing thoughtfully. "I suppose it served him well in the aftermath of the coup."

"I suppose."

"I know he still harbors regret for...well, for many things I don't know. I still don't fully remember what happened to me that night." Zandra studied the piece of sausage on her fork and frowned. "Diamandis has not filled me in, and I have not asked. I suppose I should be more curious, but I think I'd rather not know. I'd rather focus on my future." She smiled then, patting her stomach with her free hand.

Katerina smiled in return. That was the attitude she needed to have: focus on her future, on her children.

But Zandra kept talking. "The difference is, Diamandis knows. He remembers. He won't speak of it. Not to me. Not to Lysias. He's made some vague comments about not being fully in charge in the days after, but mostly he keeps everything that happened to him, everything he felt and still feels, under a very protective armor."

Katerina was reminded of their night. The night they had conceived the twins, when he'd started this whole journey with a kiss. Because she had caught a glimpse of some of his feelings about his childhood tragedy. He had been brought to his knees by the possibility of Zandra being alive, of the woman Lysias had brought to Kalyva truly being his sister.

I do not know how to bear it if it is true, he had said. He voice had been rough. He'd clearly been holding on by a tiny thread. *If it is a lie, vengeance is the only answer.*

But Katerina had seen through his anger. She should have kept her observations to herself, but seeing him so close to breaking had stripped her of caution.

You don't think it's a lie.

He'd looked at her, pain so evident in his dark gaze, when usually he never let his emotions show.

No. I do not.

She'd crossed the room to him then, not knowing what else to do. She had firmly told herself it was a *friendly* hug.

And it had been. At first.

He had let her comfort him, and even with everything that happened, even knowing that she should wish it different in the here and now, she cherished those moments where he had shown her some piece of himself that he did not show anyone else.

"I don't think he will ever truly be at peace until he deals with it," Zandra said. "Until he tells someone."

Katerina did not disagree, but she understood what Zandra was getting at. She understood that *she* should be the one to press, because Zandra thought she was a wife to Diamandis like Zandra was a wife to Lysias. That theirs was a union with love at its core. "I think you might misunderstand our relationship, Princess." She tried to smile, as if to say it did not matter or that it was for the best.

Zandra studied her for much longer than Katerina felt was comfortable. Or necessary. As though she saw right through the gentle smile.

"He allows no one speak to him the way you do," Zandra said thoughtfully. "Except maybe me." She shrugged, but her sharp, assessing gaze did not match the careless gesture. "Perhaps *you* misunderstand your relationship."

And Katerina had no idea what to say to that.

None at all.

CHAPTER EIGHT

DIAMANDIS SAT THROUGH yet another tedious meeting, then moved to the next—this one about tomorrow's ceremony and reception. It would be an all-day affair intended to allow the citizens of Kalyva to feel part of the new royal family.

Family.

Every time they said this word, something inside of him tensed, until his shoulders ached and his head pounded.

He needed to collect Katerina before he headed into the next meeting, as they would be going over a few last-minute details she needed to know.

He could have sent his assistant—useless as the fool was. He could have asked one of his staff members who *was* competent. But there was something he'd been putting off.

The ring. It sat in his pocket like a hot poker, and he felt a searing pain every time he thought about it. There were other options of course, but...

It was what his mother would have expected. And yes, she was long gone and would never know the difference. Even if she were still here, she would not approve of the way he'd handled this marriage—or of all that had happened to make it a necessity. So, to worry about it seemed wholly pointless.

But for the past few days, during which Marias had repeatedly informed him that Katerina not wearing a ring was causing whispers, Diamandis had tried to convince himself that he could use any of the other family jewels as an engagement ring. He'd put different ones in his pocket with the express purpose of giving them to her.

And never once pulled the trigger because his idiotic conscience wouldn't let him.

His mother would have loved Katerina. Her strength and her poise. The way she was never afraid to stand up to him.

So he'd retrieved his mother's engagement ring. The one his father had designed especially for her.

It had put him in a foul mood—which had already been accomplished by Katerina breakfasting before him, taking lunch in her rooms, and basically avoiding him.

He wanted to believe it was because she didn't trust herself to keep her hands off him after her ridiculous decision to keep things professional, but he wasn't so conceited. He knew it was more than that.

But then again, he wasn't so humble as to think the heat between them had *nothing* to do with it.

He reached her rooms and opened the doors to the grand sitting room. She was seated at a table in front of a large, ornate mirror. She had two women with her whom he did not recognize, and Stelios, a royal aide who usually worked in event planning.

"Oh, hello, Diamandis," Katerina said casually as her assorted attendants curtsied and bowed as Katerina should also have done. "You'll have to forgive me for not hopping to my feet, I'm feeling quite large today," she said, as if reading the disapproval he'd attempted to keep off his face.

Before he could respond, she pointed to Stelios. "Stelios has just accepted the position as my assistant."

"A fine choice," Diamandis said, with a slight nod to Stelios. He would have preferred her to have *asked* permission rather than *made* such decisions, but a queen had to have some autonomy—or so his mother had always said.

Diamandis was just not used to sharing any of the power or control that came with his position.

"Would you all give us a moment of privacy?" he asked of the staff.

More curtsies, bows, quick murmurs of *Of course, Your Majesty* echoed through the room, and then the staff slipped away as if they'd never been there.

"I think I will be quite irritated if your assistant ends up being better than mine," Diamandis said in an effort to be pleasant so he could give her the ring before he was tempted to pick an argument out of bad temper.

"You should have chosen Stelios for yourself."

"I was a bit concerned that working so closely with his husband might distract him from the tasks at hand."

Katerina shrugged. Smugly, he thought. "It will be your loss for not trusting him and Christos."

She attempted to get out of the chair, but clearly had not been facetious earlier when she had said that she was struggling today.

He helped her to her feet, and then because his attraction to her was a magnet he had not yet learned how to fend off, did not drop her hands. He kept her there, close enough to catch the scent of her delicate perfume.

She did not quite meet his gaze as she stood very still, looking at a spot behind him on the wall. She did not attempt to wrench her hands free. She just stood there and waited.

He should give her the ring, but instead, he dropped her hands in irritation.

"I am almost ready," she said, turning to a little table and picking up a pair of earrings. She studied herself in the full-length mirror as she attached one.

She wore a simple, casual dress that she might have worn when she was his assistant—complete with sensible flat shoes that had to be for comfort rather than any kind of fashion statement. But the dress was the kind of soft, stretchy material that hugged the swell of her stomach.

He had to step back toward the door as he was afraid he would reach out and touch her, demand of her what she had already refused.

"The meeting about titles should be interesting, but it got me thinking that there are some gaps in my knowledge regarding the history of the Agonas reign."

"You can always utilize the family library or Zandra's tutor if there's something you wish to know."

"I don't think the tutor can help me with this subject," she said. She turned to the mirror and fastened her other earing. She studied her reflection, then turned very slowly to look at him with an expression he couldn't read. "What happened the night of the coup?"

The blood in his veins turned to ice. He didn't *mean* to take a step back, but found himself closer to the door than he had been all the same. He had to work very

hard to make certain his voice was commanding and not…affected. "Why would you ask me this?"

"I am to be queen. I think I should have a slightly better understanding of the events than dry facts taught in history books. Even Zandra doesn't know what really happened, and she was there."

"The history books will tell you all there is to know." All anyone ever needed to know. He *wished* it were all he knew.

"The fact you won't speak of it makes me believe there *is* more to know."

He did not retreat any farther, did not allow himself to clasp his hands behind his back as he wished. He simply stood still and stared her down.

She did not blink. She didn't so much as nod her head in deference. There was a certain kind of warmth in her expression. It reminded him of the look in her eye that had led him down the dangerous path that had ultimately brought them to this moment.

She had shown him empathy, and he had forgotten his imperative control. He would not again.

"It does not matter what you believe, Katerina," he returned coldly. "It matters only what I say is fact— this will always be so. You may be the future queen, but my will supersedes yours."

Her mouth firmed, anger flashing in her eyes, but when she spoke, it was with her usual calm assistant's demeanor.

But she is your assistant no more.

"Even you cannot make your feelings facts, Diamandis. King, queen or commoner."

"You are both soon-to-be queen and commoner, and what you feel does not signify."

She smiled, but there was no warmth in it. All the warmth had drained out of her.

Because you wanted it to.

"Yes, you have made it quite clear that my feelings—that no one's feelings—matter. Here, there or anywhere. What we need to clarify, however, is that while you might see the role of queen as simply to push out the children you don't want, with no emotional connection whatsoever, *I* see it as a responsibility. And that requires *some* understanding of what happened during the most fraught time in our kingdom's history."

"How easily it has become *our*," he said, the seething anger he had to control forming something like a red haze in his vision. "You would *dare* speak to *me* of responsibility?"

"Yes. I would," she returned, as though his anger did not affect her in the least. "I know you fancy yourself the most responsible and important person in all the land, and better than everyone, but the fact of the matter is that the backbone of all that responsibility is your staff—of which I was once part. Of which I was once in charge."

Even in his anger he could not argue with her. She had been that, and more. So he chose his best weapon and defense: detached disapproval.

"We do not have time for you to pick a fight, Katerina. We have meetings and things to accomplish so that tomorrow goes off without a hitch. If you'd like to throw a childish tantrum, perhaps you can wait until our honeymoon."

"Oh, is there to be a honeymoon?" she returned acidly. "Even though I refuse to share your bed?"

"But of course. We must give the people the fairy

tale they desire." He smiled at her, and knew the small, petty feeling of having won was not conducive to achieving his goals; knew that his temper was causing him to be…antagonistic.

But she had poked at old wounds, and he only knew how to strike—hard and fast—to keep them from swallowing him whole.

Katerina blamed herself for the fact that this had devolved into an argument when she'd only been trying to reach him beneath his armor. She knew how to handle him better than this, and she shouldn't have let Zandra's words fool her into thinking otherwise. She had known he would use his cool demeanor as defense against the question. She had known this would not be an easy topic to broach.

She had *known*.

And still she'd dived in headfirst as though this were the first time she had been faced with the challenge of Diamandis and his trauma. Hands off. No entry. The end.

They could give the kingdom a fairy tale, but it would never be true.

Because although Katerina might create her own little fairy tales in her imagination, Zandra was wrong. Diamandis did not care for her feelings or for her at all. She was a vessel and no more. Perhaps because he'd once respected and appreciated her work, she could be some kind of pseudo assistant, too, but that was all. Trying for more was as futile as trying to escape him had been.

"We should not be late for our meeting."

"No," he agreed, but he did not move to open the

door. Instead, he moved toward her again. She tried very hard to remain still. Tried to harden her heart against him. Because his temper might poke at her own, but she was always weak enough in the aftermath to feel sorry for him and how little he seemed capable of dealing with his many issues.

"I wished to speak to you alone so I could give you your engagement band. It is an oversight that Marias has insisted I rectify before the public questions it." He pulled out a small box from his pocket, flipped open the lid and held it out to her.

She stared at the sparkling band. There were many encrusted jewels, but no large centerpiece as she might have expected a royal engagement ring to have. It also didn't look like any of the royal jewelry she was familiar with. "This isn't a piece I recognize."

"No. This was my mother's personal engagement band."

Katerina sucked in a sharp breath. This was…unexpected. It was the antithesis to the fight they'd just had. But he took her hand and slid the ring onto her finger. "It is what the people would expect," he said flatly.

He did not look at her, and Katerina knew him well enough to know that though he might sound flat, stiff or detached, he was working hard to perfect his mask of emotionless indifference.

What the people would expect.

Katerina wasn't sure she agreed with that. The *people* would expect fancy royal jewels—and this ring was of course beautiful and elegant and royal, but it wasn't one of the well-known pieces that centuries of royals had worn.

This was personal. His mother's *personal* engagement ring. His mother, whom he'd lost so tragically. And Katerina knew, because of all the things he never said, that he must have loved his mother very much. So all her anger and frustration with him leaked out of her in one go.

He was getting his way, steamrolling her into this life she had not wanted. He was demanding and commanding and antagonistic.

And yet so many things she knew he didn't deal with were wrapped up in this marriage—memories and family. She had seen him fall apart over getting his sister back after years of seeing him only as a lonely, stoic figure. That had been a shock. *That* had been the moment she'd realized there was a beating heart underneath all that ice.

He preferred the ice, and he would fight tooth and nail to keep it. But when so much pain was underneath, how could she not understand that? How could she not empathize with him?

He still held her hand in his though the ring was long since settled on her finger. He stared at it, a very perplexed expression on his face she did not fully understand. It didn't appear as simple as regret, but she wondered if he did wish he could take it back now that it was on her finger.

"Are you sure this is the ring you wish me to have?" she asked gently.

He kept his gaze on the ring, then slowly released her hand. He stepped back, clasped his hands behind his back, and looked at her with vague detachment.

"My mother would have liked you. Very much."

The compliment had the strength to make tears threaten. Queen Agathe had been a beloved figure in

Kalyva, so it would have been a compliment no matter what. But to have Diamandis say it to her meant something deeper. The heart she was trying so hard to protect felt bruised.

And ached for him. "Why?"

"You are practical and reasonable and kind. All things she was and which she valued."

"Diamandis..."

"Come, we are already late, and this is not a good look." He turned abruptly and opened the door. He held it open and did not look back at her as he waited for her to exit.

And Katerina had no words, no way to articulate all she felt, all she wanted for him and from him. So she said nothing, and walked out the door.

CHAPTER NINE

DIAMANDIS DREAMED OF his mother. It was an excruciating pain he hadn't suffered in years. One he thought he'd eradicated after that first year following her death, when she'd appeared in his dreams, just out of reach, every night.

He had learned to push his body and mind to the brink of exhaustion every day, and sleep had been mostly dreamless since.

Mostly.

It was not the best way to begin his wedding day, which would be a lengthy process that involved much smiling and bowing and performing for the people. It would at least be mentally exhausting in all the ways that would help him sleep tonight.

His wedding night.

He was getting married today. To Katerina. He would be a father in a few short months. Everything from this moment on was an irrevocable change, and he had no choice but to accept and handle them all.

He was the King of Kalyva. He had a kingdom to run and the Agonas legacy to protect. Everything else was secondary to duty. Everything else would be kept in its careful compartment.

He got out of bed and let the staff in with breakfast, messages, and all the accoutrements involved in dressing the king for his royal wedding. There would be the wedding, the procession, the royal dinner.

Then they could leave on their honeymoon. Diamandis did not let his mind drift to Katerina being there too. He pictured himself alone in the old, isolated castle on the other side of Kalyva. It would a period of respite that he rarely allowed himself.

And she would be with him, and for the aesthetics of it all, they would need to share a room.

Katerina would not like this. If she continued in her hands-off nonsense, neither would he.

But it would be done. *Likes* and *wants* did not signify, as per usual.

When Lysias arrived, dressed and pressed in a uniform befitting the husband of the princess, Diamandis excused his staff. He and Lysias could make the procession to the chapel alone. Diamandis needed some moments free of fluttering staff. He'd excuse Lysias as well if he could get away with it, but this was not custom. He would arrive at the chapel with his best man and the wedding would begin.

He only prayed that Lysias did not bring up anything significant. "I know you have said it is no great hardship, but I appreciate the swap all the same," Diamandis said, hoping to keep the conversation light.

"I'm certain I can find a way for you to pay me back," Lysias said, flashing his careless grin. Much like Zandra, the Lysias that Diamandis had been friends with as a boy, and the man he knew now, seemed like two different people.

Life had done that to Lysias, who, after the coup,

had been labeled a traitor along with his parents. This had been the doing of Diamandis's cruel advisers— Diamandis being too useless with grief to make any of the necessary decisions.

Lysias's parents had been sentenced to death for aiding a coup, and Lysias exiled at the tender age of twelve.

It was a miracle in Diamandis's mind that Lysias had been able to forgive him. Though Diamandis had not given the orders himself, even when he'd begun to realize they had been wrong, his pride had kept him from reaching out to Lysias. He had been afraid that correcting the wrong would cause more upheaval.

And the princess had still been missing. He'd been certain that even if the Balaskas family was innocent, they knew something they wouldn't tell.

Until Lysias had brought Zandra back to him, and the fact that he'd saved the princess when he'd been a boy had come to light.

Diamandis had certainly not forgiven himself for the years of suffering he had brought upon his childhood friend. If he had been stronger, he would never have let his advisers make such knee-jerk decisions.

"I hope it is not the prospect of your bride causing this expression on your face, Diamandis. The people will not feel any measure of assurance that this is a love match when you are scowling so."

Diamandis blew out a breath as they walked the length of the great hall toward the chapel. It was quiet here since most of the action was to take place in the chapel or outside the entrance. As his bodyguard, Christos was nearby, though not visible, but that was about it.

Diamandis did not wish to speak of his thoughts, not when Lysias would no doubt take it as an invitation to have a conversation Diamandis did not want, so Diamandis was vague. "I was thinking more of the past than the future."

Lysias was quiet a moment—but only for a moment. "I hesitate to give you advice, knowing how violently you reacted to that when we were boys."

"*Boys* being the operative word."

"Have you changed so much, then? Or just learned to hide that nasty temper because you had to?"

Had to. And how. "There are many things I had to do."

"Yes. There were and there are. I have no knowledge of what it is to be king, but I do know something of what it is to be a husband and soon-to-be father."

Diamandis wanted to refute both labels. He did not want them. They were being thrust upon him because he had made mistakes. Been careless. They were his *punishment*, and he would take this as he had taken all the rest. It was his due.

When Diamandis said nothing, Lysias continued on. "I spent my formative and early adult years believing everyone I loved would either die or betray me, because that was the lesson my childhood taught me, or so I thought."

Diamandis didn't stiffen. He straightened his tie that did not need straightening as they stood waiting for their signal to enter the chapel. Diamandis wished it would hurry up.

"That is not living, though. Not really. We can let our pasts define us so much that we do not really live, or we can deal with what tragedies befall us and at-

tempt to live in spite of them. I let my past be defined
by its most tragic moment, instead of remembering all
the good that also existed."

"You sound like your wife," Diamandis muttered,
because he could find no other words. He had no arguments for this. Except the one he knew his old friend
would argue with.

I do not deserve to "really" live like that.

"Yes, but I know something she does not, because
she cannot remember it. I am glad for some of it, for
her sake, but *I* remember your parents. I wish she
could remember them, and I wish you would not forget them so. Even being the most powerful people in
Kalyva, and dedicated to the throne and the Agonas
legacy, they were, at heart, kind, loving people. They
would not want their son to blindly commit himself
to the throne and nothing else. They would want you
to have what they had, and it seems to me you have
a chance for that here...if you'd let go your precon-
ceived notions of what you *have* to do, and focus on
all you *could* do."

Diamandis tried not to think about what his parents would want for him. He ignored the echoes of his
father's voice, offering advice about life. He focused
on the crown and only the crown.

Because the crown was controllable. Family and
love were not. He had learned this, locked in a dungeon, watching his father's soft spots end his life; listening to the screams of his mother, his brothers, and
being unable to save them. Neither anger nor begging
had made a difference.

His father had trusted a man he'd treated as a

brother—and that man had let the discontented political faction inside the castle walls.

When you loved, you could not protect what was
important.

When you loved, you failed. You did things that
could never come to light.

So Diamandis did not speak and did not acknowledge Lysias's words in any way. He waited for the signal, and when it came, he moved forward without ever
saying a word or even looking Lysias's way.

Because he *was* the throne. And nothing else.

Katerina was in a wedding dress adorned with lace and
jewels and surely meant for the princess, but it was now
hers. It had been altered to fit her growing belly and
her shorter frame. But it was not hers, she knew this.

Not the wedding, the husband, nor the crown. She
was an imposter.

And still, excitement fluttered in her chest. She
was to say "I do" to King Diamandis Agonas and she
shouldn't want to.

But she did.

A failing, certainly, but she was determined to be
smart about it all the same. So she stood, ready and
waiting for her cue, outside the grandiose doors of the
royal chapel.

Alone.

Oh, not really alone. Attendants milled about. Some
fussed with her dress, some with the flowers. But no
one stood by her side ready to walk her down the aisle.
Zandra would stand up with her, but because she was
the princess, she was already in the chapel with her
brother, awaiting Katerina's arrival.

So Katerina stood alone, looking at an artistic representation of an ancient Kalyvan wedding depicted on the giant doors that would soon open for her.

She had no father to walk her down the aisle, and she knew of no demand of an invite from her mother. She had no family. She definitely did not wish her mother or her father were present, but she couldn't help wishing for a friendly face. Someone to hold on to.

She smoothed her hands over her stomach. "I will always be a friendly face for you two," she whispered so the attendants didn't hear. Because she would always, *always* give her children everything she hadn't been given.

Someone behind her cleared his throat and Katerina looked over her shoulder to find Christos there.

"Your Highness." Christos gave a low bow. He straightened with a smile.

But he should be guarding Diamandis, not outside the chapel with her. "Shouldn't you be inside?"

He held out his arm. "Diamandis thought perhaps you would like a friendly face to walk with you down the aisle."

It was a kind gesture, but… "How did Diamandis know I would view you as a friendly face?" Christos was devoted to Diamandis and to the safety of the sovereign. Katerina had been friends with many of her coworkers when she was Diamandis's assistant, but Christos had been something of a father figure. Someone who felt *safe*. It was why she hadn't known who else to go to when she'd needed help escaping Kalyva months ago.

It was something *surely* Diamandis did not know, or Christos would not still be his bodyguard or driver.

"I'm afraid I confessed to helping you leave only a few days after you did. I could not stand the worry over being caught." He tucked her arm into his.

Katerina could not hide her utter shock. "And he didn't fire you?"

"I expected him to. I even offered my resignation. But he said if you were so desperate to leave, then it was the right thing to do to help. He was glad you had someone to turn to in a crisis."

Katerina couldn't make sense of that. "I do not understand him," she muttered.

"Perhaps he doesn't understand himself," Christos offered as the doors were opened—her signal to move forward. To say *I do* to Diamandis. To the kingdom of Kalyva.

She walked down the aisle, toward Diamandis. Her king. Her almost husband. Handsome in all his white and crisp royal finery, a perfect contrast to his dark features. Her heart stuttered, traitor that it was.

He'd given her his mother's engagement band. Had sent her a friendly face to walk her down the aisle as the entirety of the kingdom's eyes were on her.

He was a *good* man, underneath all those walls he'd built and the arrows he slung to protect them.

No, she did not think he understood himself—nor did he want to.

Christos bowed deeply to the king, then surrendered Katerina's arm to Diamandis. He took it, drawing her up to the altar. She felt his gaze move over her, the heat in it, carefully banked but there.

It would always be there. Could she resist it forever?

The bishop began the ceremony, but Katerina couldn't focus on the words. She watched Diamandis's face. And he didn't look away. He studied her as if he was having the same strange experience of feeling as if they were totally alone. As if they could still choose *not* to do this if they wanted.

This man frustrated her, angered her, and could be such an utter and total ass. But he'd given her more than she'd gotten from anyone else: kindness, respect, trust. He'd believed in her as his assistant, and now as his queen. He'd never once acted as though she wasn't up to the task.

Maybe he could never love her—or wouldn't allow himself to—but he had still been there for her in so many ways that no one in her life had ever been.

If anyone had gotten close enough, her mother had driven them away.

She still could. It was a chilling thought Katerina could not focus on here under the gaze of so many.

"I do," Diamandis said firmly, and this was Katerina's cue to pay attention. To respond to the bishop with the correct words so he could declare them husband and wife.

King and queen.

Forever.

And she didn't want to run away. The fear that had lived deep inside her when she'd found out she was pregnant was fully gone now. No matter what happened, he had promised himself to her. He would never break that promise. Maybe he could not be the husband or father she wanted him to be, but he would not abandon her.

He pulled her forward by the shoulders and pressed a very chaste kiss to her lips. Then he turned her to face the guests.

She was officially his queen. And this was not a punishment. It wasn't even a *job*. Here, surrounded by his family, his court, his people, she realized this was just life.

Her life.

Their life.

She would have to make the best of it.

CHAPTER TEN

THE PROCESSION AND dinner were interminable. This did not surprise Diamandis. He had little patience for grand events at the best of times, and this was not the best of times.

Katerina looked a vision. The white of her fanciful gown seemed to make the golden tones of her skin glow, and the sparkle of it all continued to catch his eye so that he seemed to be forever looking around the room for her when they were not side by side. She smiled at everyone she talked to. She ate and whispered and laughed with Zandra.

She looked happy.

And something deep inside ached to be a part of that happiness, even as he had to focus on anything else to keep the evidence of his arousal from announcing itself.

But every time he caught her eye, or turned to find her gaze on him, he saw something…different. As though she'd said "I do" and things had changed. She looked at him with…*something* in her gaze. A warmth that made him feel…

Like he was on a very dangerous precipice. One he could not allow himself to fall off.

When at last the dinner ended, and they could make their escape, he could not find Katerina at first. After asking far too many people if they'd seen her, he finally located her himself. She was huddled in a corner with Zandra and a second or third cousin on their mother's side. Zandra held a baby that must be Monika's, while Katerina stroked the baby's chubby cheek.

"It is time to leave, Your Highness," Diamandis said stiffly and awkwardly. He wanted to do so immediately, but instead found himself drawn into a conversation about his distant relative and her brood of children. Talk of solid foods and diapers seemed to delight Katerina, but he did not wish to hear any of it and finally extricated her from the conversation.

"The plane is waiting for us," he said, leading her away from the dwindling party. His staff would take care of everything else, while Zandra and Lysias made the remaining formal goodbyes.

"I would think the plane could wait for the king and queen if we so desire it," Katerina said, still with that look in her eye.

"But I do not desire it," he returned. As was custom—or was now expected because of his parents' wedding—they did not have to give a grand goodbye. They were allowed to sneak out, as lovebirds might.

He hurried his pace, eager to be away from baby talk and thoughts of lovebirds.

"In all the years I worked for you, I don't think you ever went to Anavolí," Katerina said conversationally. She was so relaxed. So calm. All the while wearing a complicated gown and being largely pregnant after a long, exhausting day she hadn't wanted in the first place.

She made no sense to him anymore. He'd always understood her as his assistant, but she'd changed the game. She seemed to have her own vision of what her new role was in his life and he didn't share it. Know it. Understand it.

And still she kept talking about Anavolí, the royal holiday castle.

"I would have thought it made-up if I had not had to handle the arrangements when your political allies wanted to use it," she continued.

"I have not been in quite some time. The demands of the throne are significant. I'm rather loath to leave now, but the kingdom expects such displays of…"

"Romance?" she supplied.

He fought the impulse to look at her. "If you wish." He led her outside. Christos offered a nod as they emerged and he led them to the car. He drove them to the airport, then personally saw to all the security measures. He even sat with the pilot while Diamandis and Katerina took seats in the cabin.

She chattered away the whole flight. About the people she'd met for the first time today, or people she'd worked with who had given her gifts and kind words. This was not any Katerina he knew, and it left him feeling oddly imbalanced.

Because, again, she looked visibly happy. She was glowing with it. This was not the woman who'd refused him in her sad little apartment in Athens. It wasn't even the woman who'd calmly told him she wanted a business partnership.

This was a new Katerina, and he wanted to laugh along with her when she told a story about Marias hitting the champagne a little too hard and tumbling out of his chair, his toupee sliding off along with him.

It had been so long since he'd truly laughed and the impulse felt odd enough to enable him to resist. Instead, he looked out the window and watched as they began their descent to the western coast of Kalyva.

"Diamandis, why did you send Christos to walk me down the aisle?"

He did not break his gaze from the view outside the window. It was dark—this area of Kalyva was largely isolated and the royal family owned enough of the land to keep people from encroaching, so there were few lights aside from the necessary ones to land the plane.

He considered her question and tried to make his answer pragmatic. "You needed someone."

"But the plan was for me to walk by myself. What changed?"

He had seen the crowd, the long aisle, and the thought of her having to face it alone had twisted him up inside.

He could hardly tell her that. "Christos suggested it."

"That's not what he told me, Diamandis."

Diamandis shrugged. "It is what happened," he lied. Easily. That was the kind of man he was, after all. Built on a lie. A secret.

She said nothing more as the plane touched down, as they were ushered off and into the car that would drive them to the castle.

Anavolí was much smaller than the royal palace. This had been built almost a century ago for a princess who had been frail, and the king at the time had thought her own more private dwelling would lengthen her life.

It had, and she had even married and had children here and so it became a popular retreat for any royal needing a rest or change of scene.

His parents had brought them here as children in the summers to play in the ocean—no lessons, no protocol. Just life. And family.

He had been back a handful of times since they'd died—mostly to prove to himself that he was stronger than any memories could ever be. But he'd been younger then. More…steadfast.

These days he knew better than to tempt the fate of a happy memory.

The drive to the castle was short, and when Diamandis helped Katerina out of the car at Anavolí, she let out a little noise of pleasure.

"Oh, isn't it lovely in the dark?" A smile curved her lips. "It glows, and you can hear the surf. It reminds me of the beaches at home."

"You grew up in Seir, yes?" he asked, rather than look at the white structure glow in the welcoming lights. Rather than be inclined to picture the bright blue water lapping at the sand just behind the building.

He would see it all soon enough when the sun rose.

She looked at him as if surprised he remembered her origins, but of course he knew which town every member of his staff was from. Even if she was no longer his staff.

Your wife. Your queen.

"Yes. I cannot say I enjoyed my childhood there, but I love the beaches. I love to swim or at least I did when I was young."

Diamandis said nothing to this information as he led her inside the castle. He had a small staff here, ready and waiting, and they led him and his wife to their bedchamber.

"I'm afraid we will have to share a room to avoid speculation or gossip on our honeymoon."

Katerina drifted through the room, toward the open balcony that looked out over the sea. "It is of no matter," she said, quite philosophically for a woman who'd been insistent they not blur lines mere days ago.

"I cannot imagine why you don't make more use of this place, Diamandis," she said, taking a deep breath of salty sea air out on the balcony.

He knew better than to join her. Safer to stay inside and watch from afar. "I considered giving it to Zandra and Lysias as a wedding gift, but I think they both rather prefer the bustle of the city. Nevertheless, it will be a fine place for them to bring their children to for summer holidays."

She turned to face him. She was shadowed, except for a slim shaft of moonlight that cut across her face. "What about us?"

"What about us?"

"Will we not do the same?"

Diamandis chose his words carefully. "We may, though often the responsibilities of the crown weigh too heavy to get away. But you could bring the children, of course, any time you wish."

She turned back to the sea. "I suppose they will have to be born first."

A small silence stretched out between them. Diamandis found himself in the strange situation of not knowing how to fill it. But he needn't have worried, for Katerina did quickly.

Not with words, though. She reached behind her

and began to pull the zipper of her dress down. "Can you help?" she asked.

"Perhaps you should step inside. I could call one of the maids—"

"No, no. Just pull the zipper down for me and I will handle everything." She stepped over the threshold and back into the main room. She turned her back to him, giving him no choice but to unzip her dress, revealing her beautiful back.

The scent of her wafted up around him, rich and floral. He stepped away and allowed her to deal with the remainder of the zipper herself. He reminded himself that she had been very clear.

"It is beautiful and should be saved for some historical thing or another. But it is very heavy and I'd like it off." The fabric slithered from her and fell to the floor with a soft *whoosh*.

Then she turned to face him, in an intricate piece of lacy lingerie that could only be meant to entice a man.

He wasn't the one who wanted to be hands-off, but…this was suspicious. "I thought you wished to remain business partners." He could not take his eyes off her—the flimsy lace, the glorious glow of her.

She nodded. "I did. I thought I could guard my heart if we did not muddle matters with a physical relationship."

He recoiled at the word *heart*, but this did not seem to stop her. It certainly did not stop his sex from jumping to life.

"But this is silly. This…compartmentalizing. Our life is our life, regardless." She removed the lace from her body to stand naked before him.

His perfect, beautiful queen.

He felt frozen, as though his very insides had detonated and he was merely a shell of the man he'd once been, with only one thought: *her*.

"I wish to be with you, my king," she said, sliding her hands up his chest and around his neck. "Here, on our wedding night. It belongs to us, after all. Not to Kalyva."

But she had said something about her heart, and this felt more dangerous. He should not allow it to happen. She had been right: business required a clear mind, and absolutely no muddying with desire.

No hearts. He *was* Kalyva. Nothing more.

Be strong. Harden your heart. Do what must be done, no matter how difficult. Resist feeling.

Resisting her would be power. It would be the smart move, and he should absolutely do it. But she was warmth and light, and she was his.

So he gave in.

His kiss was like the last time, and it singed through Katerina like the fire it was, but this was about more than lust, and she wanted to show him all she had to offer. She didn't want to put all her desire for him in one box, and all her other conflicting emotions for him in another. They were all one jumbled thing, in one box.

Tonight, she wanted to show him tenderness and care—all the things he did not want, and yet so desperately needed. Without fear. Without holding herself back.

She knew he'd sent Christos to walk her down the aisle. She knew this place meant something to him and that it hurt him to be back here. She wore his mother's ring, and she'd seen him through highs and lows.

She knew him. Good and bad.

She wanted it *all*. Making the best of everything as best she could.

So she soothed his savage hunger by rubbing her hands slowly up and down his back. By pulling her mouth from his and pressing soft, careful kisses to his cheeks. His jaw.

"What are you doing?" he rasped.

"Taking my time," she replied. She kissed along his collarbone as she unbuttoned his shirt, one by one, in a slow, careful rhythm. Unbutton. Kiss. Unbutton. Kiss. When his chest was revealed to her, she pressed herself to him, reveling in the warmth of him, in the hardness of his chest and the coarseness of his hair.

She traced her fingers over his skin, delving into ridges, smoothing over hard lines and strong muscles.

His hand curled around her neck, his thumb pressing her chin up so she had to look at him. There were storms in his dark eyes, and she wished she could be the lighthouse that led him safely to shore.

"Diamandis—" Words even she did not want to say threatened. She should be smarter than this, but...

"Do not speak," he said, the words coming out rough and pained, though she knew he thought he was being forceful and commanding. She knew he was trying to take some control of the situation because he felt like he did not have any.

Because he was afraid of what he felt happening between them—and maybe it wasn't the same as what she felt, but it was *something*. Even if he refused to acknowledge those feelings, that fear.

So she did not speak again. She nodded, and she gave herself over to him and what he wanted. While she allowed herself to feel it *all*.

His free hand slid over her shoulder, then cupped one breast, his thumb brushing over the already hardened nipple. She closed her eyes to lose herself in the sensation. She didn't want control. She didn't want to think. She only wanted to feel the pleasure move over her. She wanted to sigh and moan and groan without thought.

She wanted to give him all her responses unchecked. He bowed his head and sucked the other breast into his mouth, using his tongue to tease her until she was panting, begging, forgetting any thought she'd had of being slow and romantic.

There was too much need built up inside her. She tipped her head back, pleasure arrowing down from where he touched—licked. She pulsed with need and decided to give in to it. In to him. She decided to be the soft place for his ragged edges to land.

She gently raked her fingers through his hair while he made her shake with need. His mouth stayed on her breasts, but his hands slid down, finding the hot, needy core of her. It took nothing at all to have her exploding apart, his name on her lips.

He straightened, but she held on to him, forcing herself to open her eyes. She could tell he was trying to convince himself to step back, to put distance between them. So she led him to the bed before he could find his center of control. She pushed him onto the mattress, then straddled him, guiding the thick length of him inside her. Slow, slick, perfect. His eyes were like dark flames, his grip on her hips tight, as if she were the center of all he had.

She wanted to be.

So she moved slowly, teasing him as his eyes watched the place where they joined. He watched the long, slow slide. The slick, delicious friction.

Another peak washed over her, and she shuddered and lost all sense of rhythm, because there was too much. He was all-encompassing and she wanted to give in to all that he was.

His grip tightened, and he arched up into her, taking over. He was taking over, and she relished it. His gaze lifted to hers.

"You are mine," he growled. She knew he was lost in the moment. She knew he did not *want* her to be his.

But she was.

"Say it," he demanded, a king used to giving orders and having them obeyed.

She decided this was one order she always would. "I am yours, my king."

He took over, the pace wild as she shattered, over and over again. The crash of it all was bigger, stronger. It wracked through her, top to bottom, and when he roared out his release, she was limp, sated and happier than she'd ever been.

No matter how short-lived she knew it would be.

CHAPTER ELEVEN

DIAMANDIS STOOD ON the balcony watching the waves crash against the empty shore. The sun was just barely peeking above the watery horizon.

He had not slept.

She had done something to him. Scrambled up his insides so he had nothing safe and strong to hold on to. He could not fathom how. He only knew that it was all her fault.

I am yours, my king.

He hardened, here in the dim morning light, and knew if he went inside, she would take him. She had changed the game, and he felt powerless. And he had no idea how to get his power back.

Except…

There was always the terrible truth of what he'd done. The thing that no one knew.

Almost no one.

It would horrify her enough to keep her distance, surely. But could he risk the knowledge ever getting out? If it saved him this?

No, that would not go over well. He would simply have to be stronger. Compartmentalize better. He could play the role of dutiful husband and not feel anything.

He would simply have to be careful. Besides, soon she would no doubt be too uncomfortable to share his bed. Then she would have the children and need time to recover.

He could keep himself apart, while giving her the image of a devoted husband. Because he *was* devoted, after a fashion. He did not want her miserable. She had previously been a kind of partner. Yes, by doing her job well, but also just by…being there. He'd even realized, after she'd left and he'd found himself with a strange emptiness in his chest, that he'd rather enjoyed her company.

And had missed it when she was no longer there.

For work-related things, of course, because what else could matter? What else was there beyond Kalyva? Nothing. So it had been a strange kind of freedom to be around someone who did not *need* him to behave a certain way. A perplexing pride had come from taking care of her in small ways, as she took care of him.

It could be that way again, if he was careful. Besides, she would be a wonderful mother, warm and giving. He dared not let himself think of her holding children—their children—in her arms lest he forget the real, important thing here: she would be a good enough mother that he would not need to be involved.

The needs of the kingdom came first.

There was *only* Kalyva. Not them.

If he could find a way to make her understand the necessary lines he had drawn, perhaps this could be that partnership she had wanted, that comforting companionship he'd lost when she'd left. And all without forgoing what they enjoyed in the bedroom together…

He scrubbed his hands over his face. Hadn't he

learned anything about temptation and Katerina? About fooling himself?

He heard the soft sounds of movement and straightened. But Katerina was closer than he'd assumed, because before he could rearrange his expression to be suitably opaque, her hand slid up his back and she came to stand beside him.

"Good morning," she greeted, then yawned.

He did not allow himself to look at her. He could feel the satiny soft fabric of the flimsy nightgown she wore. It would be too much of a distraction when he was not yet on solid ground. "You should still be asleep."

"It seems you don't sleep at all."

She had her arms wrapped around his shoulder, leaning into him like she belonged there. "What is bothering you?" she asked, like this was a normal occurrence. Waking up together married. Sharing a conversation.

Knowing each other well enough to see through whatever masks they put on.

She had always seen through him far too well, but it hadn't seemed like such a threat when she was his assistant. It had seemed practical, as long as he did not give in to the attraction underneath it all.

And he hadn't, until Zandra had returned. Until everything had been upended. All these months later, he still hadn't rebuilt his defenses.

He was afraid that with Katerina by his side, he never would.

She gave him a little, encouraging squeeze. "You have carried the weight of everything since you were fourteen. *Fourteen*. No more than a boy."

"It was old enough to rule the country."

She tsked. "You were a *child*, regardless. Whether you want to accept that or not is no matter. You are a grown man now, and I don't know why you shouldn't share some of your burdens with your wife, who also happens to be the queen."

He had once shared his burdens, his grief, with all the men who had promised to help him, to support him. He had shared with the people his father had trusted, and so he had, too, by default. He'd believed everyone had his and Kalyva's best interests at heart, because he had been nothing but a black hole of grief.

And he had been taken advantage of. If he had not realized it when he did, his entire reign would have been a joke—and over long ago.

"Let us go to breakfast."

She sighed, but she did not argue. She let him go, though not before rising to her toes and brushing a kiss across his cheek. It was just a little gesture of affection, the kind he was forever telling Lysias and Zandra to do *in private*.

As though she were simply...ignoring everything he'd ever told her about what this marriage was to be. He followed her back into the room, that churning anger born of a feeling he would not acknowledge was beginning to brew.

"I do not know what you are trying to do, Katerina."

She pulled a robe on, then looked at him as if truly puzzled. "Do? I'm not trying to *do* anything, Diamandis. Except live my life and not torture myself with it." Then she studied him and smiled. "Oh, that's probably quite confusing for you." She crossed over to him and suddenly he didn't understand what was happening.

She was more like her old self, back when she'd been

his assistant: constantly challenging him and forever unbothered by whatever his reaction might be. Quite happy with her own situation, regardless of what he thought.

And then she kissed him—another quick affectionate peck—while he stood, stock-still, trying to make sense of it.

"We have made our choices, Diamandis." She said this with her hands on his shoulders and a pleasant, content look on her face. "We are married. We are to become parents. For my children, I will move forward and accept what life throws at me. And I will make the best of all of it."

"And what brought on this sunny attitude?" he returned, sounding more strained and less dismissive than he had intended.

She seemed to think his question over. "You gave me your mother's ring. You sent Christos to walk me down the aisle. I am pretending to believe my mother simply didn't care enough to show up for the wedding and cause a scene, but I have a sneaking suspicion you made sure that she could not attend and ruin it."

He stiffened because she was correct. The first night they'd returned to the castle after she'd told him about what a problem her mother was, he'd made certain to keep her far away from Katerina and the palace.

"That was not done for your benefit."

"Perhaps not. Perhaps none of it was, Diamandis. But regardless of all the reasons behind these things, you have been good and kind to me, even when I want to throttle you. That extends to when I was your assistant." Her expression sobered some, and that made something twist in his chest like pain. "I believe we can build a good life together, if you allow yourself to."

She said it with such certainty, as if her optimism could make it so. "You have clearly never had the hardships of life destroy everything, Katerina."

He thought she might take offense at that, or be hurt by it, but instead she just gazed up at him. *With pity*. She even patted his cheek like he was a poor, misguided child. "Oh, Diamandis. Life is hard, and tragedy unavoidable, but that hardly means you can't enjoy your life. In fact, I think it means you should enjoy it all the more when it is good."

"And this is good? A husband you did not want—a husband, in fact, you ran away from with the intent of keeping our children to yourself?"

His cold words had the desired effect. The warmth in her eyes cooled and she removed her hand from his cheek, but she did not step away. She did not break eye contact.

And it was in that moment he realized he'd expected her to. He'd expected her to step back, hurt and quiet, and withdraw. That was the reaction he'd wanted.

Instead, she slid her small hands over the swell of her stomach—a reminder, always, that she grew their children there. They were real, even if he could not hold them yet.

"Would you like me to apologize for the choices I made?" she asked, quite calmly, as if she would give such a thing if it was what he wanted.

He could not stop himself from scowling.

"I cannot. By leaving, I thought I was saving you, Diamandis. Not that I'm entirely selfless, just that… I did not want to be the reason you were conflicted or even more burdened than you already felt. Part of that was not wanting to deal with you in that state, but part was not wanting to see you, or to empathize with you in your suffering. I left because I could not fathom being the one to add to your burden when I had spent years trying to take some of it away."

He did not have words for this…this honesty. This…

She was lying. Tricking him. Trying to soften him for some…some reason.

Because for many years she *had* taken some of the burden off his shoulders, though he had never asked her to do it. She had always been there when he'd needed. She had been like his conscience, and she had reminded him that he was human and not a robot.

"And yes, some of the running away was brought on by the fact that I never wanted to be like my mother," she continued, the vulnerability she rarely exposed coming to the surface now. "She wanted to burden anyone she could. I don't know how many powerful men she tried to convince that I was their daughter."

This information shocked him enough to forget what he was trying to accomplish. "What do you mean?"

"Oh, she'd parade me in front of anyone she'd slept with, anyone she thought she could convince to accept paternity. She was certainly not choosy in her partners, either before I was born or after. Of course, she only ever tried to convince anyone who had money. Which leads me to believe my real father had none." She shook her head and cradled her belly with her arms, as though she would protect her children—*their* children—at any cost. He knew she would. "But I am not my mother. Of course I make mistakes, but I will love my children more than myself."

She kept using the word *love* as though it wasn't a weapon to be used against people. As though it was to be enjoyed, sought after. As though love protected when all it seemed to do in his life was destroy.

"So I am not claiming pure selflessness, Diamandis," she continued. "But I made that choice from a place of caring. For them. For you. And I made the decision to make the best of this situation out of that same feeling. First for them, and now for you. I will love the family we create in spite of you."

Then she smiled, and it was beautiful and open. As if none of that pain mattered. Because though they weren't born yet, she cradled their children in her arms. Their family. *Theirs.*

"Perhaps you could have breakfast brought up to the balcony while I get dressed. I'm starving." And with that she sailed off to the dressing rooms, leaving him wholly and utterly confused.

Katerina enjoyed her breakfast out on the patio overlooking the ocean below. She even enjoyed Diamandis's stifled discomfort. He didn't know what to do with her simply enjoying things— the *bougatsa* she couldn't seem to get enough of, the beautiful view of the lapping waves.

She knew he'd spent most of his adult life compartmentalizing. She'd done a lot of that work for him, but she was done. For the both of them. If he wanted to keep things separate from here on out, he'd have to do the work himself.

He watched her eat. At first, it was almost like he was counting every bite, but then…well, he was watching her mouth. She licked a piece of flaky pastry from her lip.

His gaze grew intense, and a tingling warmth crept through her body. Last night had been beautiful. He would scoff at such a word, she knew, but it *had* been. It had made her feel like they really could...do this marriage thing. This family thing.

Oh, he'd throw more walls up, this she knew. It was what he was best at, but maybe she had enough resilience in her to break them all down. She thought about this as she finished her breakfast, sitting back in her chair and licking her lips once more. She watched his reaction very closely.

"We shall go for a swim," he said, somewhat abruptly.

"*We* shall?"

"You said you enjoyed swimming back in Seir."

"Yes." And she'd been determined to enjoy a swim here, but she hadn't expected him to voluntarily accompany her.

"I have obtained a swimsuit for you, and some sunscreen. We should go before the heat of the afternoon." He motioned at the bedroom behind them. "Everything is laid out for you."

She did wish to swim, and if he was going to join her, all the better. So she went back inside and found a beautiful maternity suit in a pretty shade of purple, a broad hat for the sun, and a cover-up, along with sandals. His staff had thought of everything.

When she rejoined him, he too was dressed for the beach. He said nothing, but his gaze raked over her. She tried very hard not to smile. There was something incredibly enjoyable and freeing about simply accepting that she wanted him. And he wanted her, even as she lumbered down to the beach.

A section had already been set up for them with chairs and umbrellas, a little container of waters, juices and snacks. Someone had thought of everything.

Katerina looked at her husband. He was gazing at the sea, an inscrutable expression on his face.

He had come here with his family as a child, and she imagined he was trying very hard not to remember that. She couldn't help but wonder if he *should* remember. Still, she let him have his moment and she stepped into the surf. The water was cool but nice as the sun was already beating down on them.

It was strange to be in the ocean again. It had been a long time—years really—and she'd never been pregnant before, so this was a first. Her balance was different, that was for sure, and still she waded out. She felt lighter, buoyant somehow. Like she had back in those old, almost carefree summers when she'd been able to escape her mother and swim out all her feelings in the surf.

She didn't know for how long she swam, only that it was the first bit of quiet and calm—both around her and inside of her—that she'd had in a very long time. It made space for all sorts of thoughts and feelings, all centered around the man who was now her husband.

Forever.

He might not have wanted a wife or children, but he was not a man who would turn his back on them now that he had them. This was it, and—

Strong hands clasped her at the waist. "You should not be out so far."

She eyed Diamandis as he took hold of her. His expression was stern, his grip strong. Water dripped from his short, dark hair. How he managed to still look like a king in swim shorts in the middle of an ocean was beyond her.

"I am a strong swimmer, Diamandis."

"I do not care. It is not safe. Particularly in your condition."

"You mean being pregnant with your children?"

His stern frown turned disapproving. "Yes," he said tightly. "And as you are my wife, and they are my children, I will ensure you are all safe."

She did not reply to this. She had never questioned whether she would be safe with Diamandis because she had always known she would be. Just as she knew, in this moment, that he saw a long-ago night when he'd lost so much. She didn't want him to have to remember that on this pretty day at the beach.

She changed the subject. "What else do you know about me?"

His gaze sharpened, as he was brought from the past to the present. "What do you mean?"

"You know where I grew up, and it made me realize I never really thought of the advantage you have. You would have run a background check on me. Talked to my references. You probably know things about me that even I don't. Otherwise I wouldn't have been cleared to work so closely with you."

"I know where you went to school, your degree, your grades. What scholarships you received, and how quickly you paid your loans back. I know your work history. Would you like me to recite it for you like some kind of test?"

She shook her head, amused at the impatient tone of

his voice. He was humoring her and he wasn't happy about it. "What about things that wouldn't be found in an employee report?"

His gaze was all disapproval. "I do not understand this conversation, Katerina."

"I am simply curious. Should our union ever be called into question." She smiled, though this had nothing to do with anyone questioning him. "What would you tell people in order to prove that we have a marriage—?" She could not bring herself to add *born of love*. The words got lodged in her throat. "A *real* marriage."

"I would tell them I am the King of Kalyva and any *questions* could be considered treason punishable by jail time." The waves lapped around him, but he was steady, as if nothing, not even the ocean, could knock him over.

Katerina sighed heavily, even as she bobbed with the waves, the only thing keeping her in place his strong arms around her waist. "That would not be the right course of action."

"Then what would?"

"Perhaps digging to the depths of your acting abilities and pretending you might actually like me."

He scowled. "I do like you, Katerina. You would not have been my assistant for all those years if I did not."

"Because I am efficient."

"Because you are brilliant."

She had not expected that.

"I did not appreciate it back then because I did not know how badly the job could be done. You knew everything, handled everyone, and made my life easier with it."

She couldn't call it *impassioned* exactly, because he was clearly exasperated with her. Or exasperated with something. "I'm not sure any of that means more than efficient," she argued, simply because she liked the way his expression darkened even farther.

"Your favorite color is purple. You like those ridiculous tiny dogs like the ones Mrs. Markis has. You do not like olives."

She thought back to that odd first night back at the palace when he'd said he knew what she liked, and her dinner, a meal that that was traditionally served with olives, had not been. The *bougatsas* served at every breakfast since her return.

He had to have arranged in advance to get her a swimsuit for it to be here this morning. And the suit was purple—her favorite color.

Suddenly, this wasn't so enjoyable. It was weighty. It was meaningful.

"Does this answer your ridiculous question?"

It did. In more ways than he no doubt wanted it to. Because…these were all small things. Inconsequential things, really.

But they made up who she was and had no bearing on what she'd been to him as an assistant. If he'd absorbed this information…

Katerina did not really know what love was. She had never been loved. She didn't know who her father was and her mother was incapable of it. She had made friends, but it had never felt permanent. More like swimming through an ocean of people—she might stop and play, but she was never meant to remain in the water forever.

Diamandis had been loved as a child, by all accounts, but for so many years he'd spent his life with the weight of an entire kingdom on his shoulders, and no one to love him. So she did not think he knew either. She did not think he was cognizant of all these little pieces of her that he must have collected over years of her being his assistant—someone who should have mostly been beneath his notice.

"Come. You should not be in the sun much longer. You will get too warm."

"I like being warm." Or maybe she just wanted to stay in this moment where she thought, really thought, she might mean more to him than a capable assistant or accidental mother of his heirs.

"I read it isn't good for the babies."

"You read?"

"I do know how, Katerina," he said, so dryly she couldn't help but laugh.

But a heavy weight settled in with all that mirth as he led her back to the shore. Not a bad one, just an emotional one. He'd been reading about pregnancy, and it made his earlier comments about keeping his family safe that much more poignant.

Duty was at the center of all he was, this she knew, but it was not his duty to see to this all by *himself.* That was why he had a staff. The fact that he was here, the fact that he knew all those things about her was because...

He wanted to. Or couldn't help himself. Because he felt something deeper than duty.

They returned to the castle, and Katerina entered the shower feeling off-kilter.

You do not like olives. He'd said it forcefully, and she was quite certain she'd never mentioned it aloud before. It meant he had noticed that she always left olives on her plate when they were served to her.

He had to have noticed himself.

She'd always thought she was the only one who noticed anything.

She dressed for dinner, though she didn't feel particularly hungry. Instead she felt achy and unsteady, but she chalked this up to the emotional response to Diamandis somehow knowing her.

She did not need to verify that he could not have told her what Christos's favorite color was, or what Marias's food preferences were.

She walked out to the balcony where dinner was arranged. None of the dishes contained olives, though she knew Diamandis favored them and they were quite prevalent here.

At the center of the table was a bouquet. They were flowers from the wedding. On the day of, she hadn't thought much of them, but now she thought about how every year on her birthday he had presented her with a bouquet.

This was not unusual. Every member of staff received a token on their birthday. But that first birthday in the palace, he had presented her with a bouquet of hibiscus flowers.

"My favorite. How did you know?" In the moment, her words had been a joke—at least to her. She'd assumed he'd had some staff member call the florist and asked for whatever the florist thought or knew were her favorite.

But now she noticed that her bouquet contained hibiscus blooms. She looked up at him as he settled himself onto a chair.

"Who made the flower arrangements for the wedding?" she asked, failing to sound casual.

His eyebrow rose. "Beg pardon?"

"I was curious." She tried to smile, even though her heart pounded like she'd run a marathon. "Which staff member picked out the flowers for our wedding?"

"Portia ordered them, I believe. She sorted out most of the decor."

"But did she *choose* them?"

He frowned at her. "I suppose I made the final choice."

"Why?"

He shrugged, clearly finding her line of questioning bizarre. "No one else would do it."

"But why did you choose hibiscus?"

Diamandis's frown deepened. "I'm not sure I gave it much thought." He stared at the flowers, like... Like maybe he was realizing the same things *she* was realizing. All the things they'd paid attention to about each other without realizing why.

"They're my favorite," she said, with none of the humor she'd once used. This was a serious kind of confession. Almost as if it meant something...else.

He blinked. Once. An arrested kind of look swiftly flashed across his face before it was gone. "I'm sure Portia knew that."

But it wasn't Portia. It wasn't anyone else.

It was him. He knew about the olives, the flowers. He hadn't fired Christos because he'd been glad someone had taken care of her—no matter how furious he must have been at the way she'd left. He'd even gone so far as to have the man walk her down the aisle.

He *knew* her, and over the years he had cared for her

in a hundred small ways, just as she had done the same for him. She'd seen everything she'd done as merely her job as his assistant—knowing how he took his coffee, making sure seating charts did not force him to sit next to those he found insufferable, buying him birthday presents she knew he would like.

He'd always displayed what she gave him somewhere in his office.

This was not simply *assistant* work, no matter how often she'd told herself it was.

"Are you going to sit?" Diamandis asked, eyeing her speculatively. "Did you spend too much time in the sun?"

"No, I'm fine," she said. She sat down on a chair and tried to breathe normally, but she was realizing too much at once for her to handle.

It didn't surprise her to discover that she might be in love with him. That thought had plagued her for years, but it was the reality of loving him, of being married to him, of actually thinking he might love her back.

He would never say the words. She knew this as certainly as she knew the color of his eyes. And still…she had to tell him. She had to tell him here, now, as all their years together seemed to knit together and create an overwhelmingly beautiful tableau of two people who cared about each other, even when they pretended they didn't.

"Diamandis."

He looked up from his plate, a patient look on his face. It would disappear. Everything would likely disappear when she said the words, and still she said them.

"I love you."

CHAPTER TWELVE

DIAMANDIS HELD HIMSELF very still. It reminded him, oddly and discordantly, of when he'd first heard those gunshots in the castle.

He was frozen.

Because everything would change from this moment on.

No. I will not let it.

"This is…unnecessary," he managed to say, perhaps more stiffly than he'd ever said anything in his life.

She laughed. He found that as incomprehensible as her words. "Katerina, this is quite—"

"Unnecessary. Yes, you said."

Love. She could not. She had convinced herself of this foolish notion because…because…she was impressed that her bouquet had contained flowers she liked.

My favorite. How did you know?

He still remembered that moment. It was years ago. She'd received her birthday flowers—a common token of appreciation he gave all staff who might enjoy such things—and she'd smiled so beautifully, so unguardedly.

My favorite. How did you know?

And he'd looked at the bouquet and made sure, every year, that she had her hibiscus blooms.

But that was simply…it was simply what his parents had taught him to do: take care of your staff and they will take care of you.

You're something like a family, his mother had once told them.

Diamandis pushed this thought away as far as it would go. "You've been in the sun too long." He imagined he sounded quite knowledgeable, certainly not as rusty as he felt.

There had to be some reason, some rationale. She couldn't really love him. This had come from absolutely nowhere and he was certainly not worthy of such a ridiculous emotion. Not from her. Not from anyone.

"So love is a delusion brought on by sunstroke?" she returned, still with a smile.

"It might as well be."

"Oh, Diamandis. Honestly! Do you really need to be so dramatic about it?"

"Dramatic?" Offense poked through whatever other feeling had gripped him. *Fear.* No. He had nothing to fear.

He was the king, and he'd already lost everything.

"Yes, dramatic. I love you. There's no need to try and discredit my feelings. They are mine. I tried to guard my heart—quite valiantly, if I do say so myself. But I could not, because my heart was already yours long before that night in your office." She moved to him and put her hand on his chest, looking up at him through inky lashes. "I love you, Diamandis. I know you will not reciprocate this feeling. I think you might even believe you're incapable of it."

Love. He had never anticipated this from her. Not today. Not ever. She was too practical. Too rational. She knew him too well.

He could not do this. He could not give in to her words. It would be weakness and could not possibly end well. This was the lesson of his life.

"You do not know me, Katerina." There was a darkness inside him that no one knew.

She shook her head. "I know you better than anyone, I think. And I love you. I'm not sure it was a choice, but it *was* my choice to say that to you. To accept it. To accept everything that has happened."

It was impossible. "You will not repeat this." Love was a weakness for people like him. And she did not know him. Not the way he knew her. She would never understand the dark pit inside of him.

"You do not get to command what I *say*, Diamandis. Or what I feel. If you wish to continue on as if you do not love me, that is *your* choice. But I have made mine."

"I am the king."

"And I am the queen. I will say it whenever I wish, but let us agree here and now—I do not require any response from you. These are my feelings, Diamandis. If they seem confrontational to you, that is your problem."

"I have no problems, *glyko mou.*"

"Neither do I." She smiled sweetly at him, and he did not understand one second of this.

So he decided to ignore it. He ate his dinner, said nothing more of love, and when they were faced with their bed that evening, he gave in to his desires. Yet again.

He was not so arrogant as to promise himself he

would not give in to her, time and time again. But his feelings? He would *never* give in to those.

They did not speak of the conversation for the next few days, and Katerina did not push it. She had said her piece—what more was there? Instead, she set about enjoying the rest of her honeymoon.

And it was truly a honeymoon. They swam every day. Diamandis liked to swim straight lines, clock his time. It was exercise for him. She preferred to splash him, sit in the shallow waves, dig her fingers and toes into the sand and watch the birds swoop down into the surf.

She could be practical and focused—it was what made her a fantastic assistant. She enjoyed order, but she also enjoyed taking a break from it.

Diamandis should as well.

She could not allow herself to think she would get through his many walls. She could not believe a loving marriage was on the other side of this, but if she could get him to smile on occasion, if she could get his shoulders to relax when they were alone, would this be enough?

They ate lazy meals outside, the sun bronzing them both. He timed how long they spent in the sun, noticed how much water she drank, always so cognizant of her well-being. She knew that in his head it was about protecting his heirs.

She knew that in his heart, in a way he wouldn't acknowledge, it was about love.

If she did not drift too close to personal topics, or love, he would even laugh and converse with her and not retreat to a room on the excuse of *royal business* he could not specify.

So she did not push. She did not bring up those off-limit topics. She loved him in every way she could imagine—in their bedroom, on the balcony, at the beach. She let him have her in whatever ways he wished, given her ever-growing stomach.

Each day of that was harder than the last. The more she allowed herself to feel love, the harder it was to be met with endless stoicism, even though she knew it was the only response he'd ever give.

But she would endure it. Whatever it took. Because while he never said *I love you*, he also never said *I do not love you*.

One night, with the stars shining above them as they ate a cold meal on the grand patio that sloped down to the beach, soft music lilting through the air from the invisible speakers, she stood, held out her hand to him and said, "Dance with me, my king."

There were few things he refused when she called him *my king*. Still, there was a pause. That flash of distrust.

Because he did not trust her love, nor any casual showing of it. Passion he accepted, but gentleness he saw as the enemy. Her heart ached for what he must have suffered at such a formative age to make him so suspicious of a soft feeling.

But he rose and took her hand. He pulled her close as they swayed to the music, their bodies in perfect tune. He held one of her hands in his, the other slid down the curve of her spine. She knew what he wanted, but she couldn't help herself. She wanted something more first.

"I have been thinking about names," she informed him somewhat abruptly.

The hand on her back stopped its lazy trail downward. He did not drop her hand, but maybe that was because she held on so tight.

"There isn't much to think about. There is royal protocol to follow," he said stiffly.

"Yes, Zandra and I discussed the customs with her tutor. I am not opposed to the tradition exactly, but surely there's some wiggle room."

"I assure you, when it comes to the heir to the throne, there is no wiggle room," he returned in that supercilious way that tempted her into a smile. She should not find his arrogance amusing or attractive, she supposed, but what kind of king would he be if he did not have *some* degree of arrogance?

"The twins should have a name that *means* something. The tradition of naming them after grandparents seems foolish when naming them after your parents or siblings would be more meaningful."

"No," he said flatly, with icy coldness. He even took a step away from her, but she held on.

"Very well, but the custom includes the queen choosing one name from her own family for the fifth name, but there are no relations I'd particularly want our children to be named after. And your royal names are so long. Perhaps we could just *skip* a fifth name."

"And have our children be singled out in the history books as the ones who did not get a full name?"

She huffed out an irritated breath. "Diamandis. Honestly. You cannot possibly think anyone would notice or care."

His gaze moved from the ocean to her, and he surveyed her as if she'd grown a second head. "They are the heirs to the Kalyva crown, Katerina. Every Kalyva citizen will notice *and* care."

She had not given it the consideration that he had, clearly. Even disagreeing with him, she was warmed by the thought he must have put into their children's names.

And she supposed she could hardly argue with his feelings on the matter. He was the royal one. He knew what kind of attention he would receive, and had always received, as heir. But... "They will still be children before they are heirs."

"You cannot separate the two things," he said, with a hint of ardentness that surprised her. "If you do..." But he didn't finish that sentence, just let it trail off into silence.

She got the impression his mind had traveled to something else. Some *time* else. He looked so troubled.

"If you do, what?" she asked gently, trying to bring him back to the present, since surely that emotional response meant he was lost in the maze of his past that he kept locked away.

"If you do not wish to choose a name from your family, simply choose one you like," he said, building back that formidable mask of his. "And if you insist on not doing that, we will have Zandra choose."

"Not you?"

His mouth firmed. He said nothing.

"You haven't even asked," she said softly, even though she'd meant to swallow down the words. The hurt.

"Asked what?"

She studied him. His gaze was on the dark ocean,

even as they swayed to the music. Was he impossible to reach? "What sex the babies will be."

"I assumed the doctor would have told me if it was known." He did not look at her.

He did not step away from her.

She'd had no idea how hard it would be to exist in this place, where he neither reached out nor pulled away. Where she did all the work, and he was just... a statue.

"Do you not care to know?"

"Apparently you do not."

Katerina had considered whether she'd wanted to find out beforehand, but she liked the mystery of it. Now she studied Diamandis's face and wondered. "Would it make it feel more real to you? If you knew? If they had names already picked out?"

"I do not know what you mean. There is nothing to feel. They are real. They are why we are here."

He was being purposefully obtuse. Anger and irritation stirred within her, but that would not get her what she wanted.

What do you want? Because he has made it quite clear he will not love you.

She pushed that voice away. It sounded too much like her mother.

"You can feel one of their feet," she said, taking his hand and pressing it to where the baby's foot was lodged hard against her side. It was painful at times, but she reveled in tracing the shape of it, knowing it had to be an elbow or a foot. Perhaps a knee.

She wanted Diamandis to feel some connection to the lives inside of her. She needed in this moment to reach him in a way she hadn't yet.

He did not pull his hand away, though she felt his entire body's resistance. But whoever in there was currently trying to kick his or her way out chose that moment to move.

Diamandis jerked in surprise, though he did not pull his hand away. "It moved."

"They do that. More and more."

He flattened his hand, moving with the roll of whatever body part was pushing against her. "It seems impossible," he murmured.

"Even though I can feel them in there, rolling about, it still seems impossible to me too."

She watched him and the emotions that moved over his face. She saw a kind of wonder that she felt so deeply herself it made her want to cry. She reached up and cupped his cheek with her hand. His gaze moved from her stomach to her eyes.

"They are real and they are ours," she murmured, needing to get that through to him. They were not heirs. Not problems to be solved. They were their *babies*. Maybe she could accept that he would never love her, if she could get him to love his children…

His hand stayed on her stomach, following the movement of whichever baby was snuggled up to her right side. When he pulled his hand away, she couldn't simply let him go. She reached out, pulled him close and pressed her mouth to his.

The kiss was soft, needy maybe. But not the sexual kind of need. It was the need a heart felt when it had been alone too long. When it had been unloved too long.

She knew. She had been both.

And so had he.

As if he read these thoughts, or felt that same connection, he broke away from her. He stepped away. "I cannot." He shook his head, turning his back to her. "I cannot do this with you any longer."

"Do what, Diamandis?"

He gripped the railing of the balcony, head bowed, as if the weight of it was too much to bear.

"We will return to the palace tomorrow," he said, his voice ragged. But he straightened and collected himself, put that mask back into place. "We will go back to the way you said you wanted it. A business partnership. Nothing more."

The pain was searing, but not just her own. That he would deny himself... That he could not allow himself any...moment of connection. She could drown in that pain, or she could see it for what it really was.

"You realize this only proves that you love me."

"I do not care what it proves, Katerina. This is how it must be."

"I will still love you, Diamandis." She tried to sound calm, but she was afraid it all came out sounding rather desperate. "You cannot push me away far enough to change that. It is not for you to change. I will love you. No matter what."

He did not look back at her, but she could see that his chin had come up as he released the railing. "We will both come to regret that," he said, then strode away, leaving her on the balcony.

Alone.

It was a painfully familiar feeling in Katerina's life.

CHAPTER THIRTEEN

THE FLIGHT BACK to Kalyva was quiet. Diamandis expected anger or some sort of reaction from Katerina, but she remained stoic.

Which was good. Stoicism was an excellent trait in a queen. She would need it in spades.

So why do you feel guilty? Again?

Diamandis scowled out of the window as the palace came into view through the clouds. He had done what he could stand. What was necessary.

He had felt the movement. A life growing inside of her. *Two* lives.

They will still be children before they are heirs.

He had been given that—a childhood. And he had not been prepared, not really, for all that had suddenly landed on his shoulders at fourteen. Though it was no fault of his parents, he could hardly allow the same thing to happen to his children.

The plane landed and Diamandis was sure this heavy, dark burden inside of him was simply relief at being back where he belonged. Where he could take care of his kingdom and get some distance from his wife.

Before they could even unbuckle their seat belts, Christos appeared.

"Your Majesty." He bowed to Diamandis, but his gaze darted to Katerina before he nodded toward the exit. "There are some…concerns about our arrival that I wish to speak to you about in private. Perhaps you and I can disembark first."

"And leave Katerina behind?"

There was something strange in his bodyguard's expression, something that put Diamandis on high alert. "All right." He stood, but so did Katerina.

"What is it you want to keep from me?" she demanded.

"Just a few details, Your Highness. No need to worry." Christos smiled at her. But she clearly didn't believe it any more than Diamandis did.

"Is something wrong?" Katerina asked, curling a protective arm around her belly.

Diamandis could still feel the baby move under his hands. *His* baby. Flesh and bone. But this was not the pressing matter.

"I assure you, Your Highness. This is simply…official palace business." Christos pointed Diamandis to the door, but Katerina grabbed onto his arm.

"I do not believe you, Christos. If there is something of importance going on, I should know about it. I am the queen. You can't just shut me out because it might be unsavory."

Diamandis should probably insist she obey, insist she do this *his* way and stay here while he and Christos had their private discussion, but he was tired and he wanted—*needed*—to be away from her.

You realize this only proves that you love me.

Maybe it did. Maybe he did. But that did not mean he had to give in to it. He simply had to get away, and letting Katerina have her way in this would make that happen more quickly.

"What is the issue, Christos?"

Christos straightened. "The queen's...mother has arrived at the palace. She has been..." Christos cleared his throat. "Difficult, at best, but the staff do not want to cause any sort of...dustup."

Diamandis was shocked. He had paid the woman a small fortune to keep her distance. It had been nothing to him to ensure Katerina's peace for the wedding. And now this woman dared show her face after taking what he had offered?

Irritation bubbled through him, but when he looked over at Katerina's pale face, something much darker threaded with irritation.

"Thank you, Christos, for the warning."

"She's quite adamant she won't leave without..." He simply trailed off.

"Without throwing a tantrum?" Katerina supplied coolly. "Yes, she's quite good at those. I'm sure it will be embarrassing." She turned her gaze to him, chin lifted, skin paler than he'd ever seen it. Her eyes seemed devoid of everything, including life. "I will handle this."

He was surprised at how her reaction lit a fiery fury within him. That anyone could have caused this reaction from her was beyond unacceptable. "No, *I* will handle this," he said firmly.

"She is my mother."

"Yes, and I am the king." He took her arm and nodded to Christos. "Have the staff move her to my office. We will be there shortly."

Christos bowed and left, and Diamandis led Katerina off the plane and into the car. She was silent as they made the short drive to the palace. When he helped her out and escorted her inside, he gave her hand a squeeze.

"You are exhausted and no doubt hungry. You will go to your rooms and rest. I will handle your mother."

"I know you think that because you stopped her from coming to the wedding you can handle her, but I assure you, Diamandis, you should not be alone with her. Trust me on this."

"How—"

"I don't need to know what you did to keep her away. I only know she would have been there to ruin things if someone had not interceded. I warned you about her, so it had to be you. But you simply cannot underestimate the damage she can cause."

"I am the king, Katerina. What can she do to me?"

But this was clearly no comfort. She shook her head. "I will go with you. It is not up for discussion." And with this, she strode forward, even though he was supposed to lead her into his office.

But Katerina entered first, breeching protocol. A tall, willowy blonde stood up from the little settee. She adjusted her hat and turned to face them.

"Mother." Katerina greeted her with no inflection in her voice.

"There you are, Katerina." The woman wafted toward Katerina, arms outstretched. Diamandis watched in surprise as Katerina seemed to shrink in on herself. He'd never seen her look quite so…small.

She did not return her mother's hug, though she didn't fight it off either. She stood there stiffly, her green eyes oddly blank. He was not certain he'd ever seen her quite so disassociated from what was happening around her. It was a feeling, a coping mechanism he understood so well because...

He used it almost every day. And it was fine for him, *right* for him and his many sins, but he could not stand to see it in Katerina. He wished to whisk her away from this woman who would suck all the light right out of her.

Her own mother.

"Your Majesty," Ghavriella greeted, though she did not curtsy as she should have.

Diamandis said nothing in return. He needed to combat his temper before he dealt with this...contemptible creature.

"Is there a reason you're here, Mother?" Katerina said. There was no emotional response in her words, merely a kind of bland, detached politeness she'd often trotted out as his assistant when dealing with difficult people.

Including him.

That darkness deep inside twisted harder because no doubt he deserved it. He was no better than her mother.

You could be...

"I thought you both should know the truth, lest it come up at an...inopportune time. I don't suppose we could perhaps have this conversation over lunch?"

"I'm afraid that won't be possible today, Ms. Floros," Diamandis said before Katerina could respond. No matter what, he would not allow this woman to be under the palace roof any longer than necessary.

"Well, surely your wife's mother qualifies for a stay in the palace?"

"We will be quite happy to make arrangements for

you." *But not in the palace* was left unsaid, but he could tell by the flash of temper in her green eyes—eyes that matched Katerina's—that she understood the slight.

"What truth did you wish us to know, Ms. Floros? I assure you, the throne will handle whatever it is with the necessary action."

"Action?" She let out a little laugh. "Well, good luck with that, I suppose. We can't all bag kings." Ghavriella sent Katerina a nasty little smile. "I guess you really *were* watching and learning, no matter what you said."

There was a flash in Katerina's gaze then, but it passed quickly. Banked. Hidden. Diamandis wished he could save her from whatever pathetic ploy this was, but she was determined to see it through. So he'd do what he could to hurry the woman along.

"I'm afraid Katerina and I have important business to attend to. Perhaps you'd like to share your information with Katerina's assistant, and we can go from there."

"I doubt Katerina wants her assistant to know who her biological father is," Ghavriella said, examining her nails.

He expected Katerina to have some reaction to that, but she seemed as detached and uninterested as ever.

"It *will* come out now, I fear. Better we control the narrative, don't you think?"

"You have claimed many men as my father over the years. Why should I believe it this time?" Katerina asked.

"Because it is a secret I have tried to keep by using

those other men. No one wants their daughter's father to be a jailed traitor, after all."

Diamandis had been on the receiving end of many attempts at manipulation since he had been made king. In those early days, he had fallen for far too many. These days, he did not let them win.

But a cold dread coiled tightly within him. "Is this a generic traitor or…?"

"Thropos Palia."

Katerina thought maybe she'd heard that name before, but couldn't remember when or where. One look at Diamandis told her that *he* knew the name.

Katerina had been determined to be unaffected. It would just be another lie. Something to get under her skin—no, not even that. It would be something that would get Ghavriella the attention she so craved. From a powerful man.

The *most* powerful man.

She'd have to think about Katerina at all to care about getting under her skin.

"I mean, the king marrying the daughter of one of the men responsible for his parents' deaths is quite a story, don't you think?"

Katerina tried so very hard not to react outwardly. Her mother thrived on emotional reactions. But Katerina understood now where she'd heard that name.

Thropos Palia had been one of the ringleaders of the coup that had led to the murders of Diamandis's family.

"It sounds like you do not quite have your story straight, Ms. Floros. While Thropos was involved in the coup, he was hardly the ringleader," Diamandis said, calm as ever. "It also seems odd timing to bring this to my attention *now*."

Katerina was glad for him in this moment because she did not feel calm. She felt...too many things to name.

She turned slowly to her husband and tried to keep her tone very careful—anything to avoid giving her mother the reaction she wanted. Simply a truth. "It isn't true, Diamandis. No matter what she says, it's never true."

"I'm sure we could have it authenticated, Katerina. Thropos is still alive in some Grecian jail, is he not? A king such as yourself could get the necessary tests taken care of, and quickly, I assume."

Katerina whipped her gaze to her mother. It was a tactical mistake, but Ghavriella had never once, in all her many attempts at claiming paternity for her daughter, offered to have it authenticated. Usually when questions of validity came up, she wailed and threw massive tantrums.

Anything to get what she desired, which was always more about attention than money—though she quite enjoyed monetary payoffs as well.

"And for what reason would we have such a story authenticated?" Diamandis asked, raising a skeptical brow. "He is indeed in prison. Where he will stay. He has no claim over me or my wife, regardless. Pardon me if I do not say this tactfully, but it seems you are creating problems where there are none, Ms. Floros."

"But you are wrong." Ghavriella smiled. Coldly. "If you'll excuse me for saying so, Your Majesty. I told him. Many years ago. Back then he wanted nothing

to do with her as she had nothing to offer. But now...
well, now she has quite a bit to offer. Doesn't she?"

A heavy silence followed. Or Katerina assumed it
was silence. Her heart thundered so hard inside of her
chest it was a wonder the sound didn't fill up the room.
A pain twisted inside of her, all the way down into her
abdomen. She smoothed her hand over her stomach,
trying to breathe through this.

She had warned him, hadn't she? Her mother ru-
ined everything. Always. Even things that didn't need
ruining.

Diamandis had already pushed her away. She was
his queen in name only, and still her mother would
take that little shred of what they'd shared and try to
destroy it.

Diamandis took Katerina's hand in his, squeezing
until she met his gaze. "It has been a long trip this
morning. Go and rest." He brushed a kiss over her
knuckles.

"She is lying." She had to be. But there was a small
bubble of fear all the same. That this would be the time
her mother didn't lie. This would hurt more than all the
lies that had come before—and there had been many,
many wounds before this one.

He nodded. "We will certainly get to the bottom of
it." Then he gave her a reassuring smile and nodded to
someone. She was ushered away by the staff, led up-
stairs to her rooms and fussed over.

One of her maids even tucked her into bed like she
was a child. Only, her own mother had certainly never
done such a thing in Katerina's memory. Her childhood
had been about surviving Ghavriella's whims.

And now she was here to ruin everything, just like always.

But Diamandis had said he would handle it. That he would get to the bottom of it. No one in her life had ever offered those things, and she knew she was looking for heartache if she trusted it, but she was so exhausted. Everything hurt. She just wanted to cry herself to sleep.

So she did.

CHAPTER FOURTEEN

DIAMANDIS DEALT WITH Ghavriella in the same way he dealt with any scheming beggar. He smiled, he nodded politely, and then had her escorted to a private residence away from the palace where she would be waited on and watched while he decided what to do.

He wanted to check on Katerina, but that would have to wait. These allegations were serious. Diamandis did not think they were true—why not bring them up when he'd first approached her about staying away? But that didn't mean Ghavriella couldn't attempt to make them a problem, true or not.

Because what Katerina's mother clearly wanted was some kind of spectacle. Katerina had warned him of that herself.

So he met with Marias. He could not meet with the entire council over such a potentially dramatic situation, but his oldest adviser and a man who had counseled his father could surely be trusted to keep this information quiet and offer Diamandis appropriate advice on how to proceed.

He knew Diamandis's deepest secret, after all.

"This is a disaster, Diamandis," Marias said firmly

in response. "You cannot be married to the daughter of a traitor."

Diamandis had expected disappointment and irritation. He had been prepared for these emotions he tried to avoid, but they were not his actions and he could not undo the simple facts.

"We do not know this as truth, and I am inclined to believe it is deceit. However, we will verify if it's accurate. What I'm looking for is advice on how to deal with Ms. Floros."

Marias shook his head. "She is a disaster. You cannot be married to her."

Frustration welled up within Diamandis, but he shoved it away. "I *am* married to Katerina, regardless."

Marias said nothing, as if…

Diamandis laughed. Not kindly. "Are you suggesting I divorce her? Make my children bastards? Put such a black mark on the throne simply because a known liar and schemer wishes to make a splash? Do not answer those questions, because surely you cannot be so stupid."

Marias's eyes narrowed. "Be careful, my boy."

But the fact Marias could even *consider*… There was no *careful* to be had. "I am your king, not your boy, Marias. A man of your experience and steadfastness to the crown should know better than to overreact to a minor challenge. And anything that would change the fact that Katerina is my wife and the mother of my children is an overreaction."

Marias shook his head. "You are going to make mistakes because of this woman. You already are. Just like your father once did."

And we all know what happened to him.

Those words had always echoed in his head after a lecture, without Marias needing to say them. Because he had said them years ago, to great effect.

Diamandis could not fathom why this made him think of Katerina's reaction to her mother. The way she had tried so hard to be stoic but had been affected by the woman's manipulations all the same. She had endeavored to give no reaction, but in the end she had reacted in just the way Ghavriella wanted.

How could she not? They were very powerful manipulations.

For the first time, Diamandis considered Marias's words—not for how much he agreed with them or not, but for how much they were the appropriate thing to say to a fourteen-year-old who'd just lost his parents and siblings, regardless of his royal responsibilities.

Just like your father had become a curse, when his father had been nothing like Katerina's parents. His father had been good and noble and *kind.* More concerned about Diamandis the person than Diamandis the future king.

It had been wrong. Diamandis believed that... But Katerina's words were there. *They will still be children before they are heirs.* The feel of his child moving underneath his hand... Would being a cold, remote father really be better for those babies than being the father Diamandis had had?

Conflict brewed in his heart, like a great chasm widening down the center of him. He looked at the man he'd trusted for so long, desperate for a clearer answer. "What mistakes did my father make, Marias?"

"Excuse me?"

"I have been told, time and time again, since the

day I became king that his death was his own doing. For trusting people, for caring for people. Maybe this is true, but I find I am of an age, about to become a father myself, that I require more information. When you all natter on about the mistakes my father made, which specific ones are you referring to?"

Marias sputtered. "He put his trust in all the wrong people."

"He put his trust in you. Are you the wrong people?"

Marias straightened himself, puffing out his chest. Anger flashed in his eyes. It was not the first time Diamandis had openly defied him. It would hardly be the last, but there was something about his anger in this moment that did not match the situation. That landed in Diamandis all wrong.

Before, Diamandis had only ever thought of himself. What he felt. What a failure he was to his father's memory, and how much he wished he could change the past.

When had that changed? When had he begun to look to the future? When had he begun to look at his former self with some amount of separation—as if the boy he'd been was a different person to the man he'd become?

He had a very bad feeling that he knew the answer to that.

"Let us not worry ourselves about weakness. What we need now is strength, Your Majesty. That strength you were very good at until *she* came along."

She. As if Katerina were the problem. In fact, she was indeed proving to be a problem for Diamandis, but he did not like Marias taking the liberty of questioning the situation. Ever. He did not like any of the ways Marias was reacting today. In this strange new mindset, everything Marias said felt wrong. "What are you try-ing to hide by not answering a very simple question?"

"We have real problems, Your Majesty. Current, imperative problems to deal with. If the press catches wind of the identity of Ms. Floros's father—"

"She is no longer Ms. Floros. She is your queen, Marias. Should the press catch wind of it, then I will hold you personally responsible for the leak."

Marias snapped his mouth shut. He stood there, clearly at a complete and utter loss. Diamandis found he too was at a loss, because he did not know how to take counsel from this man now that he had all these new questions in his head.

"When you are ready to discuss the specifics of my father's weaknesses and mistakes, perhaps I will be ready to listen to your advice. As it stands now, I will act under my own counsel, and only my own counsel."

"As you did on the day of the coup?" Marias de-manded.

Diamandis held himself very still. He never thought of that day, of that specific moment. He never thought of the secret only he and Marias knew.

But Marias liked to bring it up, didn't he? It was a form of manipulation, just like the ones Katerina's mother resorted to. Using the thing that hurt him to get the behavior Marias wanted.

You're overreacting. Marias has been a steadfast adviser who cares about the crown.

But Diamandis's father had cared about *him*.

"Perhaps, Marias. But I am no longer a boy of four-teen." *A boy.* He had been a boy. Katerina had said that, and he'd argued with her. He had been old enough to be a king, old enough to rule a country.

A child, she had said.

He found it hard to disagree with her, here in this moment. The adult that he was, making the choices that needed making for the woman he— For his queen.

"We are done here. If you cannot endeavor to find it within yourself to offer advice that protects the queen as well as the king, then perhaps it is time you resign."

Diamandis left Marias sputtering and arguing. There was too much to do, and yet… He wanted to discuss this with Katerina. He wanted to find out what *she* wanted to do. She had always given him sound advice as his assistant, and now as his queen.

It had been foolish to seek Marias's help in the first place. Marias's responsibility was to ensure the crown remained respected in the eyes of the people, not to consider Katerina's feelings.

If you are considering Katerina's feelings over what might happen to the crown, then Marias is probably right, and the results will be disastrous.

Just like your father.

It was that old curse he'd lived with as a weight on his shoulders, loving his father all the same. Marias being incapable or unwilling to point out one clear mistake had left Diamandis on shaky ground.

What was his father's mistake? Was it trusting his brother-in-law? Was it ignoring his council advisers? Was it loving his wife? His children? What was this grand mistake? Diamandis needed to know so he could avoid it.

He could not figure out what was happening inside of him, what was shifting. Why was he now questioning things he'd previously always seen as fact? In all his years as king, he had never once allowed himself to look back with compassion at the fourteen-year-old who had made mistakes that had ended people's lives.

But there was something wholly life-altering about Katerina wanting to share his burdens. Something… absolving about her loving him. How had she separated the boy he had been from the man he was now with a simple word on a balcony at Anavolí?

Seeing her with her mother, seeing the way she had changed into someone else entirely had thrown him. No, not someone else. A child. A child who had never been loved or protected. A child whom everyone had failed.

He wanted to reach across time and fix that for her, but he could not. If there was anything in this off-kilter moment he knew for sure, it was that you could not erase or fix the past. He could only fix this moment.

When he strode into Katerina's set of rooms, Stelios and one of Katerina's maids were cleaning up a tea service and whispering about something.

They both stopped immediately, curtsied and bowed. In the silence, Diamandis could hear the sounds of muffled sobs.

"The queen has requested some time alone, Your Majesty," Stelios said firmly.

Diamandis could hear her crying all the way out here, and she wanted to be alone? No. "You are both dismissed," he said, already across the room and pushing open the door.

Katerina was curled up on the bed, though she pushed herself into a sitting position when he entered. Her face was red, her eyes puffy, and her hair a mess.

"Please, Diamandis, leave me be," she said, her voice scratchy.

But it reminded him of a moment he'd long since forgotten, when he'd been small—so small his brothers had not yet been born. He had snuck into his parents' room at night after bedtime. He could not remember why all these years later, because what he'd stumbled onto had stopped him cold.

His mother had been sitting on the edge of the bed, crying into her hands. His father had gone to sit next to her, pulling her into his chest, holding her, whispering soothing words to her.

He'd been so shaken by his mother's tears that he'd crept back to his room, crawled into bed and forgotten whatever it was he'd wanted her for.

His mother had been crying, and it had shaken his world. There was so much that little boy had not known or understood, and there was all the pain and heartache that was yet to come. He did not like to think of himself as a boy. He had no trouble blaming the obnoxious teenager he had been, but not that scared little boy.

It was harder to blame the boy for all of life's cruelties.

All these years later, he didn't know what his mother had been upset about, and there was no one to ask. But maybe the point wasn't *what* she'd been upset about. The point was that her husband had sat down next to her and comforted her.

So Diamandis did what his father had done.

And look what happened to him.

He had been murdered in cold blood. But that was no personal failing. How had Diamandis spent all these years believing it was? Was Marias to blame? Himself? Something or someone else?

He did not know. He only knew he could not let his wife cry all by herself.

He crossed to the bed and sat next to Katerina, gathering her up into his arms. He didn't say anything—there was nothing to be said.

He just held her.

Katerina tried to get a hold of herself. Surely she could manage that so they could focus on the problem at hand and solve it.

But Diamandis had pulled her into the warmth of him. He held her there, stroking her hair. He didn't tell her not to cry.

He simply held her.

Which made her cry harder, but she didn't mind so much. Not here in this comforting cocoon. It was a kind of release to cry, but it was so much better to say all that had been bottled up inside of her with nowhere to go for so long.

"I wish I didn't have a father. Or a mother. I'd rather be an orphan. Which probably is very insensitive of me. I know how much you loved your parents and wish they were here."

"I did. I do. But my loss does not mean you should have to love the parents you were given."

"When we got married, and she wasn't there, I allowed myself to think I was finally free. I will never be free of her. As long as she can use me as a pawn, she will." Katerina forced herself to look at him, though her eyes were puffy and her head ached. She must look a fright, but she met his gaze because he had to understand. "And now you. She will never stop, Diamandis. No matter how many times you beat her at her own game. As long as she thinks she might get some scrap of attention from a powerful man, she will make your life hell."

He studied her intently for a very long time, no doubt cataloging all the stupid ways she'd fallen apart. But he stroked her hair one more time and wiped tears off her face with his own hands, oh so gently.

"I am the king of Kalyva. No one can make my life hell without my permission, *glyko mou*."

Well, that must be nice, she wanted to say. But she just rested her head on his shoulder. She was all cried out. Exhausted. But she knew from experience that now it was all out, she would be able to think about the situation rationally and clearly.

She would find the best option for moving forward. She would somehow save Diamandis from her mother's manipulations. She had to, for his sake. For her children's sake.

"Do not worry. I will gather myself and figure out a way to deal with her." She lifted her head and tried to pull away, but he did not let her go. He studied her.

"It is a weak threat at best. If there is a story here, it will be a blip. Even if it is true, you did not grow up with the man. One could hardly connect your life to his. But I do not think it is true, my queen."

"The truth won't matter if she has her way, Diamandis. Zandra did not grow up in the palace, yet we welcomed her home—and rightfully so. She is the princess, and she deserved to return home. But people did not care who she was or whom she had been raised by. They cared that she was your father's daughter."

"It is not the same."

"It will be, for some people."

"I do not care about some people. One cannot be universally loved. Even Zandra has her detractors. This is not the goal. The goal is to ensure that the nasty words are pointless and do not turn into violent dissent against us as a family. I do not believe something like this can cause the kind of uproar your mother would no doubt like."

"Maybe not, but she'll only keep trying."

"Your mother is a cruel, selfish woman."

She had heard this all her life. Maybe not in those words, but so many people had tried to impress upon her that while her mother was quite awful, it wasn't Katerina's responsibility to bear. Cut her mother out, let it all go.

She wished she could. She wished she knew how. Diamandis would expect her to be that strong, and she could not be. Still, she forced herself to nod and smile. "Yes, I know. I shouldn't let her get to me."

But Diamandis's mouth firmed in confusion. "Of course she gets to you. She has betrayed you, time and time again. This is not so easy to forgive and forget. Not from anyone, but especially not from a mother."

He spoke from experience, she could hear it in the conviction of his words. He would not speak like this if he had not been betrayed by someone close to him, which made little sense considering his family had been murdered and he let few others close.

"Who betrayed you?"

He sucked in a breath and let it out slowly as he looked away. "I have betrayed many."

She didn't think that was true, but even if it was…
"Not me, Diamandis. Never me."

His eyes searched her face, and she held very still.
She wanted this to be the moment he gave in. She
wanted it to be the moment he understood what they
could have if he'd only let his past go.

But she also knew, based on her reaction to her
mother, that she had not let her own past go. So who
was she to hope the same for him when his past was
all the more traumatic?

"Why do you always seek to absolve me, Katerina?
Even before, when you were my assistant. I am an arrogant, inflexible ogre, but you have always insisted I
am better than I really am."

"You are a bit of an ogre," she agreed, chuckling
when he glared at her. "And underneath all those
quirks, I suppose, is a man who guards a soft heart
because of a tragedy that marks him still. I absolve
you because I know where these behaviors come from,
and I know you could do better if you could realize
that those past mistakes don't define you. I love the
man you are, Diamandis, regardless of those things
you think make your heart black."

"There are things I have done that you do not know
about, that no amount of love can absolve."

She knew this. She knew that there were things,
things from the night of the coup, that he held on to.
Secrets he wished to take to the grave. Secrets that it
would change him to confess. "Tell me," she whispered, desperate to be the one who got through to him.

But whatever moment she thought they might have
dissolved before her eyes. His gaze went very blank.

He brushed a kiss over her forehead, but there was no real warmth to it. Maybe kindness, but not love.

He gently pressed her into the pillow as he stood. "Rest, my queen. I will handle everything with your mother."

No one had ever said these words to her before. She looked at him, wishing it were that easy. Wishing she could believe him. Wishing...

He had comforted her. He had held her while she cried. When she thought he would have turned away or scolded her for such a foolish emotional outburst.

He'd absolved her too.

And if they could give each other that, maybe there was hope for them even in the shadow of her mother's accusations.

But only if Diamandis put down his heavy burdens, and that seemed even less likely than getting rid of her mother for good.

CHAPTER FIFTEEN

DIAMANDIS IGNORED MESSAGES from Marias over the next few days. Though most of them were apologetic, Diamandis had no time to decide how he felt about his adviser. About the things changing inside of him.

He had only one concern: to find a way to keep Ghavriella Floros away from Katerina for the rest of her days, regardless of the veracity of her claims.

So he consulted a man he knew could outmaneuver an operator like Ghavriella and was relieved when not two days later Lysias came to him with answers.

"It pays to have a billionaire for a brother-in-law," Lysias said, not waiting for Diamandis's ever-missing assistant to announce him.

Diamandis looked up from his desk as Lysias sauntered in. Though Lysias was irreverent and obnoxious within the palace walls, he could be counted on to act with decorum in public, and Diamandis was learning to accept this.

Slowly.

"I should hope so," Diamandis returned, which caused Lysias to chuckle as he lowered himself onto the chair opposite Diamandis's desk.

"Ghavriella and I have a friend in common—your former royal doctor."

Diamandis scowled. The former royal doctor had been prepared to falsify Zandra's DNA results for Lysias and had consequently been relieved of his position.

"It appears they both met with Thropos in the prison in Athens *after* the wedding. I leaned on the good doctor a bit and he admitted Ghavriella was attempting to forge your wife's paternity—something Thropos was willing to be in on, hoping it might gain him some measure of clemency."

Something dark and hot welled up inside Diamandis. It was an old feeling of betrayal he often tried to squelch with ice lest it get...out of hand. His hand curled in a fist as he tried to manage his temper. "Did she really think she'd get away with this?"

"I don't see why not. It's not so difficult, particularly if the person you're doing it to doesn't know what you're up to. I had once planned to forge Zandra's paternity. I would most certainly have gotten away with it."

"You say that with such ease, as if you don't feel guilty in the least."

Lysias shrugged as if the betrayal he'd almost enacted mattered not at all. "I don't."

Diamandis would never understand the man who had once been as close as a brother and was now his actual brother-in-law. "Why not?"

"Well, for starters, I didn't go through with it. If I held myself accountable for everything I thought about doing or almost did, I would be depressed all the time. Oh, is that your problem?"

Diamandis spared Lysias a cool look, but the man only smiled wider. It had eased some of the anger inside of him though. The scheming woman had been caught in time to do no further damage to Katerina.

This time.

"She wished to cause a ruckus. No doubt she will try again."

"Yes, but if she's attempting to forge records, it's likely she knows who the father is and wants no one to know. I know you have men on her, but I can put one of mine on her for the foreseeable future as well, should she seek to find a new target when she realizes this one will not work."

Diamandis nodded. It was something, and while he could keep one of his own men on the case, Lysias tended to have a staff that was a little bit more…rough around the edges. Which was exactly what he needed.

But this made him think of the doctor, of Marias's questionable loyalties, the councilmembers he'd had to dismiss—all the men who'd used him in the past under the guise of caring for the Kalyvan crown.

"Am I such a bad judge of character?" Diamandis muttered, not having meant to say it out loud. But the past few months had been a constantly humbling exercise in sifting through all the staff members he thought had been on his side purely because they had been on his father's.

"You are in a difficult position, Diamandis. People have used the memory of your parents for their own ends, including myself. Anyone who truly knows you doesn't blame you for this."

"Perhaps *someone* should blame me."

"I think you do that enough all on your own."

Diamandis had had quite enough of Lysias. He nodded to the door in dismissal. "Thank you. This will indeed protect the Agonas legacy." Diamandis considered it a dismissal, but Lysias continued to sit there, studying him.

"You wish to protect your *wife*, not your legacy."

"She is the queen of that legacy."

"Hmm."

Diamandis stood. He needed no more of Lysias's poking. He had the information he needed and he would use it to protect his legacy, which just happened to include Katerina. "That will be all, Lysias."

"Unfortunately, there is one more thing I'd like to discuss with you as a member of the council. Marias isn't happy."

"And I am not happy with Marias, so I suppose that makes us even."

"He's been spending an inordinate amount of time sucking up to Zandra these past two days, and in ways that make me realize previous overtures since her return might not have been quite so genuine. He claims his reasons are lost time and wishing to see his beloved king's children supported and happy, but there is something I do not trust about the man."

"You yourself told me Marias was not one of the people who would have voted against me."

"Yes, but only because there was no one to replace you. Now that Zandra is confirmed to be the princess, it feels…questionable. Especially considering he doesn't approve of Katerina."

"He doesn't approve of *you*."

"But he does approve of my bank account."

Diamandis shook his head. He already had his

own doubts about Marias, but how could the man he'd trusted for so long be working against him? "Marias was like a father to me. I would not have succeeded without him."

"But did he step into that role because he wished to support you, because he loved you like a son, or because it gave *him* power?"

Diamandis could only stand there in silence. His own suspicions had been drowned out by his feelings. By his loyalty to Marias. He had talked himself out of those very questions without ever answering them.

But Lysias voicing them…

"I am an outsider, of course. I have no idea what happened that night aside from what little I saw on my end of it. It is Zandra's belief that you are the only one who fully knows what happened."

No, not only him. Marias and him. The secret keepers. *For the good of the kingdom. If anyone found out…*

Lysias did not take Diamandis's silence as a hint to leave. He just kept at it. "But Marias's words and attempt to ingratiate himself with my wife make me wonder if that is true."

Diamandis's head whipped up to glare at Lysias. "What do you mean?"

Lysias stood. "I don't have details or evidence or information. I have vague suspicions. Just keep in mind, Diamandis, that secrets have more power than the truth ever will. And it has taken some time, and some doing, and your sister's love, to get to a point where I have forgiven you for the role you played in my parents' murder. Because you were a boy who had been traumatized, and the adults who should have cared for you instead used the tragedy to seize power."

Everyone kept talking about how much of a boy he'd been, but the kingdom had expected him to become king. He had been expected to rule. How could everyone now decide he'd been *just a boy*?

"I got rid of everyone who had a hand in the aftermath. Anyone who voted for your parents to be executed without sufficient evidence. No one involved is still in my employ."

"Are you so certain?" Lysias asked gently.

Gentle enough it felt like a dagger. Because no, he was no longer certain. He just was too torn up to do anything about it. And what kind of king did that make him?

Just like your father. Who will die this time?

"As I said, I do not have any proof, but I could get it," Lysias said carefully. "With your permission."

"And without it?"

"I would not stick my nose into it. As long as there seems to be no danger to my wife. It is not my goal to upend your life, to discover if Marias is an enemy, unless you want answers."

Diamandis tried to keep his breathing even, tried to work through all that roiled through him. He didn't want to poke into it. He wanted to tell Lysias to forget all this foolishness. Marias had been good, had gotten him this far. Secrets weren't powerful. They were *necessary*.

But it was as if Katerina were here beside him because he knew what her advice would be. What she would tell him to do.

She had never trusted Marias.

"You have my permission."

Katerina had spent some time after her mother's appearance wallowing. It turned out that wallowing as a queen was quite nice. People waited on you. You didn't need to get out of bed in order to eat your weight in cookies. If you said you didn't want to do anything, you didn't have to do anything except sit in a cocoon of blankets and pillows and feel sorry for yourself.

But she couldn't indulge herself for long. She was too used to *doing.* Restlessness pushed her out of bed and in search of work. Stelios was far too competent an assistant to leave her much to do, so she'd cornered Tomás and commandeered some of *his* assignments.

She didn't think Diamandis would approve, exactly, but he had made himself scarce after her emotional breakdown and who could blame him? She'd likely be able to do some work to help out Tomás without Diamandis ever—

"Your Highness? The king," one of her maids said at the door.

Well, *that* figured.

Diamandis strode into the little sitting room where she'd been doing her work. He frowned at the tablet in front of her. "What are you working on?"

"Well, I needed to occupy my mind with something, and Tomás left your appointment log in such a mess that I took it upon myself to fix it."

"You are not my assistant any longer," he said, though not as disapprovingly as she might have expected.

She turned in the chair and gave him an arch look. "I am better than Tomás."

"A tree would be better than Tomás."

Katerina shook her head, trying not to smile. "Why do you keep him around?"

"I have not had time to hire a new assistant. No one compares to you, Katerina."

His words shouldn't please her as much as they did. "I could still handle *some* of my old duties. Obviously it wouldn't do for the queen to answer phones or deal with dry cleaning, but I could handle some things. I could certainly attempt to train the young man."

"Soon you will have enough to handle," he said, nodding toward her stomach.

She looked down at it, placing her hand over the bump. "Yes, I suppose." She rubbed at the little twinge she felt there, and then looked at her husband. "I haven't seen much of you."

He sighed. "I tasked Lysias with tracking your mother's activities to see if she's been up to anything, and it appears Lysias discovered that she was attempting to forge a test that would prove you were Thropos's daughter, but it is not true."

Katerina did not move. It wasn't a surprise exactly. She'd been trying to accept it so she could handle it if it turned out to be true, but it was just another of her mother's cruel ploys. "I see."

"It seems she has been planning this since the wedding. The traitor is not your father, Katerina. She cannot cause harm to you in this way."

Katerina looked blankly at the wall behind him. She wished this were a relief. "She will keep trying."

He moved, then surprised her by kneeling before her and taking her hand in his. "And we will keep proving her wrong," he said, as seriously as any vow. "Lysias has put a man on her. We will watch her until her end days to ensure she has no power to harm us."

She blew out a breath, surprised at how shaky it was. She kept thinking she knew how to deal with this, but… He was the epitome of a mixed signal. And she knew that this was because he *was* a mixed signal. Inside, he was fighting a raging battle between what he truly was and what he thought he should be.

But no one had ever taken care of things for her before, and she did not know how to pretend that didn't matter. So she leaned forward and pressed her mouth to his. Just gratitude.

And love. "Thank you."

She expected him to withdraw. Comforting her was one thing, born of his innate need to solve a problem. But this moment was more than simple comfort.

She sat on the chair and he kneeled on the floor, which put them nearly at the same height. They were so close that their noses practically touched and he studied her as if she were a puzzling mystery when she knew she was not.

The true puzzle lay inside of him. And instead of putting it together, he kept pushing the pieces farther and farther away from each other.

He laid his lips on hers once more, gently. Not as if she were fragile, but…sacred. And he kissed her just like that, until she was shaking and blinking back tears.

"I thought you wanted to keep your distance," she murmured against his mouth, because while she might not resist in this moment, she could hardly ignore the fact that he'd been so quick to run away before.

"I suppose neither of us is very good at sticking to our guns when it comes to each other."

She wanted to smile, but it was different. He wanted her in his bed. She… "But I love you, Diamandis."

He did not pull away. There was something…different about him. She wished she could believe he was changing, but she wanted him to so desperately that she was afraid it was only wishful thinking on her part.

"You do not know me, Katerina," he said, so very seriously.

Which was absurd. "I worked as closely with you as anyone for years. I know who you are, Diamandis." Just as he knew her, whether he'd ever admit that to himself or not.

"But not what I have done."

He sounded so tortured, so burdened. She laid her palm against his cheek. "Then tell me. Don't walk away. Don't push it away. Tell me, Diamandis. It will change nothing."

CHAPTER SIXTEEN

DIAMANDIS'S HEART FELT as if it were trying to escape his chest. It beat hard and painfully, and it was difficult to breathe.

He wanted to tell her. He wanted to lay his sins at her feet. She was always absolving him, so why not for this too?

Please, for this too.

Lysias's words about secrets having more power than the truth rattled around inside of him. *Power.* Had everything always been about power while he'd just been trying to survive?

If he told her, she would know the secret that Marias had told him no one could ever know. But maybe if she knew it, she would stop asking more of him. Maybe *she* would keep her distance since he could not.

Maybe she would finally understand why he could not be the husband and father she clearly wanted him to be.

Maybe she will love you anyway.

This, he knew, was the most insidious thought of all, because he wanted it so desperately to be true. But he was kneeling in front of her like some kind of supplicant. Carefully, he rose. "I do not mind you doing some of Tomás's work if it pleases you," he said.

Had he really expected that to work? He didn't know, but she was on her feet, gripping his hands so he couldn't retreat farther without yanking away.

"Tell me what you have done," she said earnestly. "Tell me what you think is so horrible that I could not love you. Prove to me that you are a man who does not deserve love and happiness, Diamandis, because I will never believe it if you do not disabuse me of the notion that you are a *good* man. *I* have only ever seen the good."

She looked like such a *warrior*. Like she would take on armies, pregnant and furious. Beautiful and fierce.

He could not deny in his heart that he loved her, and likely had for a long time. He had tried—valiantly, he liked to think—to escape it. But the feeling was there. It was a poison he could not eradicate. A poison that would likely kill them both.

Love always did.

So he would have to kill the love. Even if it meant unearthing his darkest secret that he swore he would never tell a soul.

"I have committed murder."

Katerina did not gasp. She did not drop his hands and step away. She simply looked at him as though he'd said *I can fly*.

"Dearest, what on earth do you mean?"

Dearest. When he should be dear to no one.

"You and Zandra have been telling me over and over that I was *just a boy* when I became king. That I was a victim to the circumstances, though I lived and everyone I loved died or disappeared."

"Yes," Katerina agreed. "Because that is the truth. Just because you weren't murdered doesn't mean you weren't traumatized."

"And what about those who cause trauma?"

"Diamandis—"

"I murdered my uncle. Should I be excused for that too, simply because I was fourteen?"

And still she did not step away. "If the history books are true, he is the one who killed your mother."

"Vengeance, then. Vengeance is the excuse?" he demanded harshly, because she was not reacting as she should. She kept seeking to excuse him, when there was no excuse.

Marias had told him that there was no excuse. That it was an evil thing he had done. That he should have handled it better. That as king, he was not worthy, but he would have to lead anyway. Marias would show him the way.

Maybe not in those exact words, but that was the message Diamandis had received, and he did not know how to go back and view it any differently.

Katerina inhaled and then led him over to a bench where they could both sit. She drew him down next to her, never letting go of his hands. "Tell me what happened. The whole night. Let it go, Diamandis."

He withdrew his hands from her, though he did not get up and leave like he should. "I can never let it go."

"Just tell me," she insisted. "Walk me through it. Maybe I'll find a way to hate you yet."

He scowled at her because she was treating this… all wrong. She didn't think she would despise him, but she would. She had to. Marias had said…

He did not know if it was strength or weakness to

confess all, but it would solve the problem of Katerina. He was sure of it. She would keep her distance and then things could go back…

He did not know what they could go back to, but he also did not know how to resist her any longer, so he would have to give her the tools to hate him. *Please hate me.*

"My parents were shot—"

"No, Diamandis. The whole thing. From the beginning."

The beginning. He did not wish to remember or relive the beginning. That it was a day like any other. That his mother had talked excitedly at breakfast about going to Anavolí the following morning. That he had sulked because he felt he was too old and mature to splash about the beach with the children.

He did not tell Katerina those details. Could not bring himself to voice them. Achilleas and Rafail kicking each other under the table. Zandra whining about not liking eggs, and his father grinning at his mother while telling Zandra that they were very special eggs. Magical eggs.

And then any magic had died hours later.

He had been silent too long, but Katerina did not push him. She sat there, shoulder to shoulder with him, waiting patiently.

"If there was any tension beforehand, I did not know it." That was the beginning. That to him it had been a day like any other. "Zandra had been put to bed, and Achilleas and Rafail were supposed to be asleep, but had been sneaking into each other's rooms. I often did any extra studying at this time, so I was in my room. One of my father's guards and one councilman came in unannounced. They said there was some cause for alarm, and I was to go with them. I wanted to gather my brothers and sister, but they assured me they already had men on it."

He had believed them. He hadn't had a doubt in his mind that they were telling the truth. He had followed, like a lamb to sacrifice, but not slaughter.

That had been for everyone else.

"We heard gunshots before we got to the basement, but they said I would be meeting my parents and the children down there. Everything would be fine."

He could still remember how afraid he had been, because he'd been so certain he was being led to join his family in a place of safety where they already were.

"When we arrived downstairs, no one was there. No one would explain. They just told me I was safe and locked me in a room." He still remembered the dark. The soft echo of gunshots he could only barely make out. The feeling of not knowing what was going on, or where his family was.

Left alone and in the dark.

Katerina slid her arm over his back, rubbing from side to side. "I suppose they were trying to protect you."

"I thought so. It was Marias who found me, who let me out. He cautioned me to stay where I was, not wade into the chaos, but he could not tell me where my family was. I had to find them."

Then you must take this. To protect yourself. Diamandis had not questioned why Marias was carrying a gun. He'd questioned nothing because he'd only wanted to find his brothers and sister. For some reason, in that moment, he'd been so certain his father would be fine.

He was strong and invincible, and Diamandis was like him, so he would go and save his siblings like their father was no doubt saving his mother.

But he'd only found death and blood in the boys' room and nothing in Zandra's. "The boys were already dead."

Katerina rested her head on his shoulder and said nothing. In the silence it felt like the only option was to go on. To see it through. To tell Katerina what he'd never told anyone.

"Zandra appeared to be missing, so I set out to search for her. I thought maybe she was with my parents, so I doubled back to their rooms. I heard…" It haunted his dreams. His waking hours. His everything. "I heard my mother crying. Sobbing. Begging."

Bang.

Then nothing. Just what had felt like an endless moment during which Diamandis had not been able to move. Maybe if he had…

"A man all in black, carrying a large gun, stepped out of my mother's room. He turned the gun toward me, but… I shot him first." Sometimes, in his memory, it didn't make sense. The man had paused, giving Diamandis the opportunity to best him. "I shot him."

"He was going to shoot you," Katerina said.

Sometimes I wish he had.

"I left him to die."

"What were you supposed to do?"

He stood abruptly and paced away. "You do not understand." She didn't. She couldn't. If it had been anyone else, perhaps…

But Katerina was so calm. "No, I do not understand. I cannot imagine what it must be like to be forced to take a life, but you *were* forced. No one would have blamed you for this. Why would you turn this into a secret?"

But he could see Marias's face as he'd pulled back the mask of the gunman. The shock. The horror. It hadn't been just anyone.

It had been Diamandis's uncle.

Everyone will blame you for this, Diamandis. They will think their king is a murderer. This will not do. Your father never would have done something like this. He was weak, but you…

"It was my uncle. My mother's brother. I killed my own uncle."

"That does not change the circumstances around it, Diamandis. You defended yourself against a man who was going to kill you. Who killed your parents and was part of the group that killed your brothers. I'm sure that was… Of course you would feel guilt, confusion. I understand your feelings at having been forced to do such a thing, but I cannot understand why you would blame yourself for this?"

This must be our secret, Diamandis. For the good of Kalyva. For your father's name and legacy.

"Marias…" He hadn't been able to find the words. The memory seemed to have changed on him, turning Marias—his savior, the man who'd led him away and told him what to do when he'd been lost—into a villain.

Katerina's expression immediately changed. "Do not tell me that old fool had something to do with this. Oh, *that* would make sense. The ridiculous hold he has over you!"

"He has no hold over me. He did not lock me in that basement room. He let me out. You do not understand. I later learned, *from* Marias, that a few council members used the coup for their own gains. They could have stopped it, but instead my uncle gave the violent mob the means to invade the palace thinking he'd have some sway over me. Those council members who'd claimed they'd saved me, who placed the blame on Lysias and his parents, they didn't want the monarchy to be overthrown, but they wanted someone they could control. A boy. Me."

"I'm sure they did, but who says Marias didn't want to as well?"

Diamandis looked down at Katerina blindly. "But he didn't work with them. He worked *against* them. He helped me get rid of those who sought to grab power, who blamed staff for their own defections."

"Which gave him the highest place on your council and cleared out any rivals he might have among your advisers. It won him not just your trust, but your devotion. You *owed* him. He kept your secret and convinced you it was a secret no one would understand, when I think it is something that anyone would understand. Who benefits from it being a secret, Diamandis?"

"The kingdom," he said, because that had always been the answer he'd been fed. The answer he'd felt. He wasn't worthy because…

Katerina rose and crossed over to him. Her eyes were wet but her words were strong. "Think, Diamandis. Think beyond the scared, frightened boy you were, to the reality of the situation. No one would have blamed you for killing any man in self-defense, let alone the one who killed your parents. Regardless of who he was to you."

"I don't…" But he'd been having doubts about Marias, hadn't he? Could it be that the man he'd trusted was as bad as those early political graspers?

But he had killed a man. He had been too weak with grief to see through the machinations of his father's men.

Men, when you were a boy.

Are you still a boy? Are you too weak now?

He looked at Katerina, who had never led him wrong in all her years in his service, and now was his queen. Who'd never put her own needs or wants above his. He trusted her more than anyone. She understood his responsibility to the kingdom, and his father's memory. She had always been correct about things, even when he hadn't wanted her to be.

Because she was a marvel. A wonder. Beautiful and strong. *His.*

But if he loved her, then history would repeat itself. He would make concessions for her, more than he'd already made. And someone would sneak into the cracks, as his uncle had.

For a moment, he could see the pools of blood in his brothers' room, but instead of the boys, it was Katerina's lifeless body he saw. The image was fictional, but if he gave in to this, it could become real.

"Perhaps you are not wrong," he said—or tried to, but his throat was closed so tight it was hard to push out the words. "Perhaps my oldest confidant is in fact a traitor to me and the crown."

He could not trust a feeling, could he? Not when it came to anyone.

"Thank you for this clarifying discussion," he said stiffly.

Confusion chased over her face and she reached out for him. "Diamandis..."

He sidestepped her arms and began to back away toward the door. "I think you are quite right about many things."

She continued to follow him as he backed away. "I'm glad, but—"

"Marias will be dealt with swiftly as my concerns about his loyalties have been growing lately. What you've shed light on makes it clear we cannot move forward with him in my employ."

"I think that's the right course of action, but—"

"It will be a messy political business and I will be very busy. I think it's best if you return to Anavolí, with the medical team of course. Perhaps Zandra would like to join you."

Confusion was being replaced with frustration, and a little flash of anger. "I have been by your side while you've dealt with many a political mess, Diamandis. I will hardly run away now just because I am your wife or because I am pregnant."

"Politics is no longer your duty, nor is standing by my side. Your duty is to birth our children. Best if it's done away from the political storm, I think."

"Birth...? You want me to spend *months* at Anavolí without you? Have our children over there while you remain here?"

"It would be best. If I do not see you before you leave, I bid you farewell." He gave her a stiff bow.

"Diamandis, you cannot honestly—"

But her words abruptly halted because he had walked away. And never looked back.

CHAPTER SEVENTEEN

KATERINA HAD FELT many things in this palace, but confusion to this degree was new. She had *no* idea what had just happened. What Diamandis was thinking. What was behind this decision.

She was angry, yes, but she could not begin to fathom what had happened during that conversation. She had expected him to be angry and upset. She would not be surprised by self-blame or recriminations, because the men who should have protected him had manipulated him instead. They had brainwashed him into this warped vision of himself.

And still, under all that, he was a good man. No doubt forged by the parents who had loved him, and each other, so very much.

Her heart ached for Diamandis, that they had been ripped from him so cruelly. All because of a throne. All because of men and their greed for power. So many different attempts at getting what they wanted through manipulation and violence and cruelty.

Katerina rubbed the side of her stomach. The twinges had been getting more frequent, but the nurse had assured her that as long as they were not consistent, or more painful, everything was fine.

Go to Anavolí. Alone. What was he thinking? That she would *abandon* him?

But she was so tired. The pregnancy was taking a toll, and if there was going to be upheaval, then maybe…

No. She couldn't leave him. He wanted it, so she couldn't do it. She finished her work on Diamandis's appointments, ignored another uncomfortable twinge, and then asked Stelios to have a lunch brought up.

When he announced its arrival, he also announced Zandra.

"The princess has requested to eat with you, if you are up for it."

"Of course."

Zandra entered ahead of the staff with a rolling tray of food. She plopped down into a seat near Katerina. "I have heard that Diamandis wishes to send us away."

Katerina smiled at the blunt way Zandra put it, though she didn't feel particularly smiley about it.

"That is his current grand plan."

"Are you going to go along with it?" Zandra thanked the staff members once they had lunch set up, then dismissed every single one of them. Katerina waited for everyone to leave before she answered Zandra's question.

"I don't want to go, no."

"Lysias is not too keen on letting me out of his sight this far along," Zandra said, running her hand over her belly with a fond smile. "And I am not eager to leave him either, though I do want to go to Anavolí. I think I might remember it. But seeing it in person would clarify it for me. Perhaps we should all go there once Marias is dealt with."

It sounded so nice. The four of them—the family—taking a vacation together. Katerina had never imagined such a thing. And her children would have a cousin their age. They would have a true family. A kind, loving family.

What about their father?

She knew it was foolish to wish for a man to change, but surely when he saw them…

But he'd confessed everything to her, everything he thought was shameful about himself, and left. Coldly. He wanted to send her away. Anytime he felt something, he put distance between them.

It would likely be the same with the children. Perhaps worse, if familial memories made being with them even more distressing and emotional.

"Aren't you hungry?" Zandra asked when Katerina had still not made herself a plate.

Katerina shook her head. "No. The babies have been quite active in there and it doesn't do much for my appetite."

"You must keep your strength up though." She put her own plate aside and bustled around the cart making a new plate. She handed it to Katerina. "I will not leave until you've eaten at least half."

Katerina had to swallow down the lump in her throat. It was such a strange thing to be so looked after, so taken care of. Diamandis had comforted her after her mother's cruelty, and now Zandra, pregnant herself, was fussing after her and making plans for future family vacations together.

"Zandra, do you understand your brother?"

"Oh, not at all," Zandra replied emphatically. "He's a complete and utter mystery. I think Lysias is able to shed some light for me sometimes, but the man makes no sense." Zandra took a big bite of her slice of cheese. "Except, to me, it is clear Diamandis loves you very much and has for some time."

"*Is* that clear?"

"Perhaps not to you. But... I know he loves me, no matter how annoying he finds me. So I can recognize it in him, even if he can't. I can see the way he looks at you, talks to you, treats you. There is a kind of... fear in it."

If she had said anything else, anything about love or joy or sweetness, Katerina would have scoffed. But it *was* fear she saw in him, so how could she argue with Zandra? "Every time I think I have made some progress, he only pushes me farther away. I am getting tired of it. Perhaps I should accept that he only has push inside of him. Maybe..." Her throat closed and a lump formed there, but she managed to speak on. "Maybe I should go to Anavolí. Give him some space. He can deal with all this and..." Katerina trailed off because she felt so tired. So wrung-out. Maybe space *was* the only option.

"Well, it would give him time to miss you, maybe."

"You're very supportive, Princess. I don't know how to express how much I appreciate it." She rubbed her stomach, where that same old pain was lodged. Maybe one of the babies was kicking a nerve.

"Are you all right?" Zandra asked.

"Just one of my twinges."

"Twinges?"

"A little pain, here and there. Nothing consistent. Nothing to worry about." Still, this one wasn't going away quite so quickly.

"I don't have any twinges. And you're quite pale."

"Well, you only have one in there."

"Katerina, you should consult your doctor before we make any more plans to leave, don't you think?"

"We? I thought Lysias would not want to be separated from you."

"He won't, but I'm hardly letting you go by yourself. You need a friend. Lysias will stay here and talk some sense into my stubborn brother, and I will go with you. We'll take a little break for a few days and come back next week and sort everything through. Doesn't that sound good?"

"I would not count on anyone getting through to your stubborn brother if I cannot."

Zandra smiled at that. "You have always been the best at getting through to him, that is true. But maybe a little distance, a little missing you is just the ticket. Now, you stay right here. I'll have someone fetch your doctor and then we'll begin making plans, all right?"

Katerina nodded, overwhelmed by Zandra's kindness and warmth. "You don't have to go with me, really, Zandra. I appreciate—"

"I won't hear any more about it," she said, heading for the door. "We're sisters."

Sisters. Katerina had a sister. A family.

Finally.

Diamandis spent his morning going through historical records he'd never before allowed himself to consult. He got the full picture of who Marias had been to his father.

And who he had not been.

Then, he planned. At first, he did this alone, and

then, in a moment he would have once called weakness, he consulted Lysias.

"I think giving him his full retirement is too kind," Lysias said, brooding, which was rather unlike his usually irreverent brother-in-law.

"We will call it insurance over a kindness." Diamandis knew he should feel *something*, but mostly he felt numb.

The man he'd trusted was a grasping traitor. Not so overtly that he could be sent to jail, but just insidious enough to make it clear he had never been on Diamandis's side.

Ever.

A staff member announced Marias's arrival.

"Would you like me to stay?" Lysias asked. Diamandis saw it for what it was: a kind, supportive gesture between friends. Family.

When they'd been boys together, they had been close friends. Like brothers. It had taken nothing at all for Diamandis's advisers to convince him that Lysias was a traitor to the crown, deserving of any bad thing that happened to him.

"I have not been a good friend to you."

"I think the same could be said about me. Even if my attempt at revenge did reunite you with your sister, I assure you it was purely accidental."

But it did not feel like an accident. It felt like a second chance. "I would like this to change."

"Well, Diamandis, we aren't just friends anymore. We are brothers."

Brothers.

Diamandis nodded. "I appreciate the offer to stay, but I feel as though this is something I'd rather do on my own. Perhaps…perhaps we should have a family dinner tonight. The four of us."

Lysias bowed. "Gladly, Your Majesty."

And he only sounded a *little* mocking as he said it. He took his leave and Diamandis gave the signal for Marias to be sent in.

Marias entered Diamandis's office with a stiff body and an inscrutable expression.

"Have a seat, Marias," Diamandis instructed, taking his own seat behind his desk. He looked down at the older man and began. "I have a few questions to ask you to determine how we should move forward at this current juncture in our working relationship."

"Very well."

"I have taken many things you said at face value over the years, Marias. I have trusted your guidance, your discretion, and your dedication to the crown."

"Yes, and you did not question it at all until you let your feelings for a woman cloud your reasoning."

Diamandis raised an eyebrow but did not let his temper take over. "Perhaps," he agreed equitably. "I'd like to discuss the coup with you."

Marias's mouth firmed. "As you wish."

"If you could go back and change anything, would you? Before, during, after?"

Marias's eyebrows drew together in confusion. "I would do whatever it took to steer your father toward an action that would have saved his life."

"Like what?"

"What do you mean?"

"What specific action would you have advised him of that you feel would have saved his life?"

Marias blinked. "Why, not trusting your uncle, of course."

"And why didn't you advise him of this in the time leading up to the coup?"

"I did. Your father did not listen because your mother begged him to give her brother a place on the council."

Diamandis would once have believed this. He looked down at the notes he'd taken as he'd gone over records. "Unfortunately, I have gone back over the council logs from the months leading up to the coup and there is, in fact, not one word spoken against my uncle by you, or anyone else." Love had not poisoned his father, not by any stretch of the imagination. "No evidence anywhere of you counseling my father to listen to his brain, not his heart."

Marias huffed and fidgeted in his chair. "They were private conversations."

"There is no evidence of any meetings you would have had with my father privately. You were merely an alternate at this time, an associate council member who spent more time in administration than in one-to-one face time with the king. Is this not true?"

Marias seethed and said nothing. Diamandis, on the other hand, felt nothing but ice all the way through.

"It makes sense why you might have wanted to ascend those ranks. Why you thought, with someone else on the throne, you might have a better chance at a higher position."

"You have let your little *wife* poison your mind."

Even then, Diamandis's temper did not jump, because of course this was not true. There were many things his feelings for Katerina might have affected, but this was not one of them. "Katerina has always been most reasonable, most levelheaded. I can see why this would be difficult to see as she has never cared for you, but she never let that sway her. I cannot say the same for you. Quite an emotional response for a man so determined I should have none."

"I do not know what it is you wish to accomplish, or what the queen or your brother-in-law wish to accomplish, but if you let these…these…*schemers* have some influence over you—"

"Neither Katerina nor Lysias has done anything but support me these past few weeks. *Me*, yes. Not the crown."

"You *are* the crown."

"I have endeavored to be, it is true. I thought I had to be that and nothing else, and perhaps I should be. But when I was fourteen, I was a boy. My parents and brothers were murdered, my sister lost to the chaos. And you, you saw an opportunity to twist and turn the whims of fate to give yourself power over me." His temper was licking at the edges of his words, but still he sat and watched Marias turn an impressive shade of purple.

"I have advised you in leading the kingdom well. I helped you oust those who blamed the wrong people, the people who sought to control you. I did what I saw fit, and I will not apologize for it."

The biggest issue was that Diamandis believed him. Marias had done what he saw fit. However, that did not make it right. "Maybe you did. But it was wrong, and it was cruel. To use my shame against me, my fear against me, my *grief* against me, all so you could determine how I would act." Diamandis looked at the portrait of his father beyond Marias's head. "I have endeavored to be a stronger king than my father, but in doing so I have made many mistakes. Including keeping everyone so far away that many were ready to vote against me just months ago."

"Not I, Your Majesty. I have always supported you."

"Because you have control over me. But no longer." Diamandis met the man's gaze. He iced the temper away and spoke calmly and clearly. "You are relieved of your position."

"You cannot fire me. I am an elected member of the council."

"You will resign."

"I will not," Marais said, punching a fist on the arm of the chair.

His temper, his panic, only aided in Diamandis keeping his calm. "You will if you wish to keep your retirement pension from the crown. You will retire, and you will leave. Otherwise, I will present what I have to the council in a bid to cancel every last benefit, honor and recompense you've received." He offered Marias a bland smile. "Do I make myself clear?"

"You will live to regret this."

"Maybe. There is always a chance of that. But I assure you, you will regret more if you should ever try to undercut my position, if you continue to make Zandra uncomfortable and my brother-in-law suspicious, if I ever hear you having said an unkind word about my wife. I will make sure you lose it all. Whether that's tomorrow or twenty years from now."

"This emotion, this insanity, it will be your end, Diamandis. Just like your father."

For so many years it had been the weapon used

against him, but Katerina had given him armor for it. She had heard all the horrible things he'd been taught to believe would ruin him and loved him anyway. Absolved him, like always.

Just as his parents had always done, and no doubt would have continued to do if they had lived. They would not like the man he'd become—cold and remote and dedicated only to the crown.

But they would love him. And in that love, there was always hope. Hope that he could change, could be better.

Diamandis looked from his father's portrait to Marias's angry face. "Perhaps it will be my end, but I have finally realized I would rather live like my father for a short while, than live like the man I've been until I am elderly." He rose. "You are dismissed, Marias. Unless you'd like to throw a fit at the next council meeting and lose everything. It is up to you." Marias sat for long past what was proper. "Your king is on his feet, Marias."

Slowly, with a face turning an ever-darkening shade of purple, Marias got to his feet. "You will regret this, and I will live out my retirement laughing at your misfortune."

"Very well." Diamandis smiled at Marias. "Do not forget to bow to your king, Marias."

The man scowled but bowed stiffly, then stalked out of the room. Diamandis knew he would have to keep an eye on the man, but the threat of losing his retirement payout was a large one. He would be bitter about this, but Diamandis did not think danger would befall them from his actions.

Marias simply wasn't brave enough to do anything in the light. Or to do it to a man rather than a boy.

Diamandis breathed in, surprised to find he felt... lighter. There was an odd sadness to the whole thing, because he had spent so long trusting Marias, but there was also something freeing in learning. Growing. Changing.

Loving.

Because he loved his wife. His sister. His brother-in-law. The family they had scrabbled together out of the ashes of tragedy. And if that meant an end to him ruling Kalyva...

So be it.

He would go to Katerina now. He would tell her he loved her. He would ask her to stay. He would endeavor to be the man his father had been. Not only a king, but a man behind the crown as well. He would change. With her help, he could. She believed in him, and wasn't she always right?

Brighter than he'd felt in decades, he skirted his desk and strode for the door, but before he reached it, it burst open and Zandra ran in.

His heart turned to ice.

"Diamandis! It's Katerina." Zandra's face was pale, and she reached out for him. "You must come at once."

CHAPTER EIGHTEEN

KATERINA HAD NEVER known such pain. Such fear. The twinges had quickly become something more, far more by the time the doctor arrived.

Still, the doctor spoke calmly as she insisted Katerina lie down and get comfortable while she checked her out. She murmured some things to a nurse who hurried out.

"Are the babies okay?" Katerina asked, worry clogging her throat and making the words hard to push out.

"We're going to get some instruments that will allow us to monitor them, but right now they're fine. It looks like you might be going into labor. Early labor is quite common with multiples," she said matter-of-factly.

"It's too early."

"It is early, but not necessarily too early. We will do what we can to stop the labor and go from there." The doctor patted her hand reassuringly. "You have the best team to help you, Your Highness. Your job right now is to rest and try to relax. I believe the princess has gone to find your husband."

Diamandis. She wanted him here. To hold her hand. To hold *her* as he had after her breakdown over her mother. But…

She knew what this would do. Any hint of loss would push him farther into his shell. He would see it as his own failure, no matter how idiotically stupid that was. "No. Please, I don't think... I don't want him in here."

The doctor was clearly perplexed by this, but she nodded. "Very well. I'll go and tell your assistant. You just lie here. Just breathe, all right?"

Katerina nodded and tried to do what the doctor said. Breathe in. Breathe out. Put the pain somewhere else. Put the worry *anywhere* else. There was pain and it was scary. All of this was scary.

She wanted someone, and if she let Diamandis in on any of it, what would be left? A tear slid down her cheek, though she would have thought herself stronger than that.

The doctor returned. "If you do not want your husband in here with you, is there someone else? Someone you can talk to in order to keep your mind off things?"

A bubble of panic welled up inside of her. *Alone. Always alone.* But that wasn't true because Zandra had said she'd go to Anavolí with her. "Princess Zandra, if she can. If she isn't busy. I..."

The doctor nodded and made a motion to a maid who quickly disappeared.

Another wave of pain swamped Katerina, and she felt something was wrong. Just wrong. Like something was leaking out of her. Like the pain was stealing her ability to breathe.

"Something's wrong," she managed to rasp. It was all wrong.

The doctor's expression got very grim. "Katerina, I need you to stay with me. I need you to fight."

There was a grayness swimming around her vision. Fight. She knew how to fight. She'd always had to fight. But this was too much. Too much pain and too much weakness. A blackness was creeping over her.

She heard her name. She heard instructions, but she stopped feeling any of the pain. She was going somewhere else.

And in the blackness, all she wanted was her husband. He had promised he would take care of things, hadn't he?

But even the king could not take care of this.

Diamandis ran through the palace, shoving his way into Katerina's rooms only to be met with Stelios and a maid blocking his way.

"Move."

Stelios shook his head. "The doctor has said the queen does not wish to see you at the moment."

It might have hurt, but he didn't feel it because fear was clawing through him. Zandra was not one to exaggerate and she had said that Katerina was not well.

"You cannot ban me from my wife's side. I am the king."

But Stelios did not budge and looked ready to fight him if he pressed. "The doctor was quite clear."

Diamandis was ready to take on such a fight, but a great commotion arose around them, both from inside the bedroom and outside the sitting room. Doors flew open and medics with a stretcher rushed forward while a nurse came out from Katerina's bedroom.

It was chaos.

And in the confusion of the chaos, Diamandis ran

forward into Katerina's bedroom. The doctor shouted orders from Katerina's bedside.

Her hands were bloody, and Katerina was still— too still—and pale.

Gone.

The blood was a visceral reminder of a past he'd worked so hard to forget. But he'd foreseen this, had he not?

Katerina and blood.

This is what love did.

"Your Majesty," the doctor said once she had instructed the medics. "I have called emergency services to transport the queen to the hospital." Katerina was moved to a stretcher. Lifeless.

"She is…dead?"

"No," the doctor said, following the medics carrying Katerina away from him.

Blood. Blood. Blood.

"Meet us at the hospital, Your Majesty. We are working hard to save all three lives. I will explain everything once she is stable."

Then they were gone. And he was in a room alone with bloody sheets.

Until his sister ran in. She was breathing heavily, her arm curled around her own rounded stomach. She should not have run. Lysias was not far behind her. Diamandis stared at both of them, neither quite making sense in the context of everything.

Blood.

"What has happened?" Zandra asked. He barely felt the hand clutching his arm. "Diamandis?"

"I have sentenced them to death."

"What?"

"Come, Diamandis," Lysias said firmly, taking his other arm. "Let us go to the hospital and wait for an update."

He did not remember anything from that moment on. It was all a blur and suddenly he was in some sterile, private waiting room of a hospital. Life and death did not care if you were royalty. Tragedy did not care if you had already seen your fill.

Lysias and Zandra took turns at his side, reassuring him that things would be fine. That the longer it took, the better prognosis there must be. If she was dead, he would know.

But they were wrong. He knew this in his soul. Even when the doctor explained that Katerina had gone into early labor. That there were complications, but they were working to deal with them.

He was not allowed to see her, so he knew.

She was dead. He was certain of it. They were all dead because he had loved them. Because he had wanted to make it all real.

And this was his payment for such foolishness.

Zandra sat next to him after the doctor left and took her hand in his. She squeezed. "Have faith, brother," she said.

"There is no faith. They are dead. It is my fault. I loved them. I have sentenced them to death."

Zandra did not move away, but he could tell she didn't understand. Couldn't. She thought he was overwrought, and he was, but Zandra could never fully understand.

"You sentenced them to death…by loving them?" she repeated. A question.

"Yes." A curse.

She was silent for a few moments, though she did not let his hand go. "Do you really think you have such power?" she asked incredulously. "Your emotions control *science*? The human body?"

He sighed heavily. "Fate, Zandra. Fate controls everything. And mine is death."

She scoffed. She *scoffed* at him! Here in the middle of yet another bloody tragedy. "We make our own fate, Diamandis, or I would have been dead in a ditch long ago. But I fought. I survived the unthinkable. It was so bad I don't even remember it, nor do I want to. And I am here, back where I rightfully belong, because I do not care about fate, and neither should you. You are the king of Kalyva."

He shook his head. She couldn't understand. "Our father…" But he could not say the words. The words Marias had programmed into him long ago. Emotion. Connection. The enemy. The beginning of an end.

And why might he have wanted to isolate you from any kind of love?

He swallowed against his tight throat. Could he really believe that when the loss of everything he'd wanted to love was so evident?

Zandra uncurled his fist, and then she put a picture in his hands. It was an old snapshot of their parents. Not a royal portrait, but one of the more casual family snapshots. Not in their royal finery, but two regular people smiling at the camera.

His mother was pregnant. With him.

"I have been carrying this with me, trying to remember them. Sometimes I think maybe I do. A word. A flash. But I guess I'll never know for sure it is them."

He tried to pull his hand away, but Zandra pressed the picture more firmly into his palm.

"Not so long ago, I looked at their portrait in your office and asked them to show you love. Maybe it's a silly thing to believe, but they brought you Katerina. Your babies. And nothing you do or don't do will change the outcome of what happens in this hospital. But you are the only one who can choose faith, love and future, Diamandis. Not fate. Not tragedy. *You.*"

He said nothing. What was there to say? His parents were dead, even as they looked back at him from this picture.

Zandra brushed a kiss across his cheek. "Lysias and I are going to go in search of food. We will be back soon."

She was lying. They could have any staff member bring them whatever food they wished. She was giving him a moment alone.

With this picture of his parents.

He stared at it, no matter how his mind screamed at him to put it away. To put this all away. To freeze himself out once again.

But his heart ached for them. For the love and support they'd given him in their too-short lives. Zandra had said she'd looked at a portrait and asked for something. She'd asked for love for him, which was foolish. Silly indeed.

But he had certainly been given it. Katerina had been steadfast in her love. Never pulling it back. Never questioning it. Katerina believed in love, in him.

Just as his parents had.

He stared at their long-gone faces.

"Not a day has gone by where I have not missed

you," he heard himself say, as if he were outside his body, watching some other person talk to a picture of dead people.

"I do not know who to beg, or to which deity I should supplicate myself. I only know you and your love. Please, please… I need her. I need *them*. If I am to be punished for loving, punish *me*." He pressed his forehead to the picture.

He heard the door open, but did not look up, assuming it was Zandra and Lysias. But someone cleared their throat.

When he looked up, it was the doctor. He leaped to his feet.

"You have two sons, Your Majesty. They are both healthy, needing only moderate interventions." She smiled at him.

He could not take this information in. Not yet. "The queen?"

"She is still fighting. You may come and meet the babies."

"I wish to see Katerina."

The doctor nodded. "Once she is stable." And she led him out of the room, down a maze of hallways, to a room with little plastic cribs. There were two nurses who curtsied upon his entrance.

The doctor guided him over to two little enclosures. "Baby A is five pounds, five ounces," the doctor said, pointing to the infant on the left. "Baby B is four pounds, eight ounces, and we're monitoring him to make sure everything is going well. But they're both healthy, Your Majesty. Very well developed for being early."

Diamandis could only nod. They were so small,

wriggling and moving about, one with his eyes open—
a dark, inky blue. The other with his eyes closed as the
wrap of blankets he was swathed in wriggled.

"In regard to names, are the royal customs to be followed?" a nurse asked.

He looked down at the two babies. Sons. *His sons.*
So tiny. So helpless. With little shocks of dark hair.
And Katerina was not here to see them. To love them.
Love.

"No," he said, surprising even himself. He had been
given twins. Just like his brothers. Names that deserved
long, happy lives.

"This is Rafail Youkilis Lysias Agonas," he said,
as the newborn scrunched up his tiny face. Diamandis
looked down at the one still being monitored. "This is
Achilleas Alexander Balaskas Agonas."

"I will make sure it is noted right away," the nurse
said, scurrying off.

"Would you like to hold them?" another nurse asked.

He would. Every cell of his body ached to hold his
children, but he needed their mother with him.

"I need to see my wife. The babies should be with
their mother."

The doctor nodded solemnly. "The queen will be
under for a while longer yet. Once she wakes, we will
have a better idea of her prognosis. But she is strong,
Your Majesty. And we will do all we can for her. You
can go and see her now, and we will bring the babies
in when we can."

Diamandis nodded. "Very well. Take me to her."

More hallways, bright and white. Curtsies as he
passed. Whispers. But nothing mattered. Only Katerina.

He was ushered into a private suite and there she

was on a bed, in the midst of a cold hospital room. Pale. Lifeless. So many monitors hooked up to her beeping and flashing, but he could see the rise and fall of her chest.

Breathing, alive. Not blood. Not death. Alive. If she breathed, there was hope. Zandra had told him to have faith. After seeing his children, he felt compelled to have all the faith in the world. Just for them.

"She will be asleep for a while yet, Your Majesty. The nurses will check periodically. You are welcome to stay as long as you like. We will work on getting the babies moved in here as soon as it is possible."

Diamandis nodded and waited for her to leave before he crossed to the bed. He knelt down next to it on the hard floor and took Katerina's limp hand.

He did not waste time, because time was always fleeting.

"I love you. My queen, my heart. If… I will be everything you need, I promise. A husband. A father. I will love you all more than life itself, but you must come back to me."

Please, he said silently, thinking of the picture of his parents in his pocket, *bring her back to me*.

CHAPTER NINETEEN

KATERINA COULD NOT quite make sense of where she was or what had happened. Something beeped obnoxiously. She felt…fuzzy and heavy and out of sorts. She could not remember where she was.

Had she made it to Anavolí? Was she ill? The babies… The babies…

But then she heard a cry. A baby's cry. And she forced her eyes to open.

The room was dim, and it hurt. Moving at all felt wrong, but there in a corner was a man. Not just any man.

Diamandis, tall and regal but looking exhausted, held a small bundle of blue in his arms. The room spun a little around him and she had to close her eyes, but when she managed to reopen them he was still there. With a baby.

Her baby. *Their* baby. She looked around wildly until her eyes dropped to the two hospital bassinets. Two. *Two.*

"Diamandis…" But her voice didn't come out as more than a rasp.

His eyes flicked to hers immediately and he crossed to her. His gaze tracked over her. "You are awake."

"Are they okay?"

"Yes. We have two sons, Katerina, and they are doing just fine despite the early entrance." He tilted the child in his arms so she could see his precious face. Dark blue eyes, tiny, tiny nose. A shock of black hair. Hers. Here. Alive.

But she was in this bed. She was…all wrong, and Diamandis looked at her as if she would disappear simply by the looking. "Am I going to die?"

He lowered himself into a chair that was positioned next to the bed. He adjusted the baby into a one-arm hold. He took her hand with his now free one. "No, *glyko mou*. I am the king and I will simply not allow it. You will be quite well and we will go home soon. Together."

She swallowed against so many things. Bits and pieces came back to her.

I will love you all more than life itself, but you must come back to me. Surely she had dreamed such passionate words? Surely it was all a dream?

"*We* will go home together?"

"Yes, I'm afraid I will not allow you to be out of my sight for quite some time." As if to prove it, his gaze tracked over her face. Then he blinked and forced his mouth to curve.

"You will be happy to know I have broken royal tradition, per your request. You told me they should have names that mean something. So I have named them after my brothers. And they only have four names, for why shouldn't history wonder why our children are so special that they will break tradition?"

She searched his face. Something had changed. She could feel it, and yet…

"You will have to wait to hold them, I'm afraid," he continued. "But it is a good enough reason to get strong, is it not?"

"Diamandis…"

"Achilleas is asleep, but he is off all the machines. I will bring him over when he wakes. But they are both fine, strapping young princes."

"Diamandis…"

She didn't know what she wanted to say, but something in his whole being simply crumpled. He lifted her hand to his mouth and pressed a kiss there, pure anguish in his gaze.

"I thought I had lost you. I could not bear the thought," he said roughly.

Her husband. Her sons. Her life and her heart. Everything was fine, and she would get better. She would make sure of it. "Everything will be all right."

He nodded and kissed her palm once more. "Katerina, I love you. I thought this was a curse. I thought I had doomed you, but Zandra reminded me that while I might be king, I do not have that kind of power."

Katerina had hoped to hear those words someday, but had mostly convinced herself they would not come, even if she knew he felt such things. Even if she thought she could get through to him. She wanted to reach out and touch him, touch her son. *Rafail.* But she couldn't seem to move in the ways she wanted.

"I suppose I had to visit with death to get this kind of confession," she said, struggling to shift in the bed.

He shook his head, his expression pained. "Because I am a fool. But I will… I will endeavor to forgive myself for the mistakes I have made, because they were made with an honest heart, if nothing else. I will endeavor to make no more, but I suppose this is life. We make mistakes. But I will never mistake this simple fact again. I love you. I want you by my side. I want to be your family, to raise our children as my parents raised theirs. Our children will know love and faith and…everything we wish them to. Together."

Tears tracked over her cheeks, but her husband wiped them away. Love and faith. Together. The family she had known they could be, if only she could get past his walls.

And now here they were. Not perfect, because she *had* nearly died, but this was life. Never perfect, but beautiful nonetheless.

Diamandis pressed a kiss to her forehead, and when Achilleas awoke, he brought the boy over so she could see him. So she could see both of her beautiful sons, in their handsome father's arms.

She had been alone so long, and now she had a family. One made of love and hope. She was proud to be the queen of Kalyva, and she was good at it. But nothing in her life would ever match the joy of loving her husband, and the pure perfection of being a mother.

A month later, finally healed and strong, Katerina requested something of her husband he almost refused to give.

"I cannot allow it, Katerina." He even glared at her.

But she sat in the chair, feeding the insatiable Achilleas, who had grown faster than anyone expected. Diamandis held Rafail, pacing, as was often the only way to get the energetic boy to sleep.

"I will see my mother, Diamandis. If you will not bring her here, I will go to her."

"Over my dead body."

Which was how, a week later, she was seated in a receiving room while Christos ushered her mother into the room. Diamandis stood behind Katerina's chair, and the boys were in another room in the care of Zandra and Lysias.

"I thought I was to meet my grandchildren."

"I made it very clear you would not be, Mother."

Ghavriella sniffed. "Then I do not understand why I am here after being treated so rudely the last time."

"You mean when you came here to lie about the paternity of your daughter," Diamandis said coolly.

Ghavriella rolled her eyes. "Honestly."

But she could clearly come up with no retort.

"I asked you to come here today, because as much as I would love for you to be a part of my children's lives, some things are going to have to change. I will not let your toxic behavior touch my children."

"Yes, I know. Such a terrible mother! So *toxic*. Feeding you, clothing you, getting you to school and back. How very *dare* I?"

Diamandis made a noise, but Katerina held up her hand. She had expected this behavior. She and Diamandis had both begun to see a family therapist to deal with their issues. They were acting today on her advice, and the driving need Katerina had felt to stand up for herself. To draw this line in the sand.

To be the adult in the situation. She did not expect the same of her mother, but she wanted to behave in a way that made herself proud.

"When you are ready to truly build a relationship with us, to join us in family therapy—"

Ghavriella made a sound of shocked outrage.

"—I will be happy to attempt to mend fences. But this is my line in the sand. You will play no part in my children's lives without this step. No matter how you scheme."

"Utterly ridiculous! I'm sure everything is all my fault. Well, I don't need you or your royal children, Katerina. I am doing just fine on my own."

Katerina did not react. She nodded at her mother. "Very well. But understand this—I will protect them from everything. I do not know why you could not do the same for me, but I understand now, truly, how very much not my fault that was." Which was why she had truly needed this moment. She had not expected her mother to change, but she had needed to bring that realization full circle.

"You have married a king and you whine at me about protection?"

Katerina kept her bland smile intact, then nodded at Christos, a signal they had agreed upon. "That is all, Mother. I hope someday you can find it within yourself to change."

Christos offered Ghavriella his arm. She looked at it, then at Katerina, then at Diamandis. She whirled away and stomped out of the room without an escort. Christos bowed to them, then followed her out, no doubt to make sure she actually left.

Katerina let out a long, slow breath. She did not feel good, but she felt settled. She had made her choices, made them clear, and shut the door without locking it forever. She had little hope her mother would change, but she would always allow for the possibility.

And she would never let her mother turn her into a small child again. Her sons and her husband had given her a strength she had not known she possessed. She would protect them from everything.

That was what today had been about. Proving that knowledge to herself. No one, not even her mother, could ever turn her into someone she did not want to be again.

She rose and Diamandis held out his arm. She took it and they silently exited the room.

"You seem content," Diamandis murmured as they walked down the hall to where their babies were. He held her arm as they walked, a thoughtless gesture these days, but that was what made it all the more beautiful.

"I am." She smiled up at him. "Sometimes you need to make a stand and create boundaries for yourself." She paused, reached up and fitted her hand to his cheek. "And you can because there are so many people who love you standing behind you."

He pressed his mouth to hers. "Always, my queen."

EPILOGUE

DIAMANDIS WATCHED HIS wife chase after their sons in the sand on the beaches of the castle at Anavolí. His childhood best friend carried his niece on his shoulders while Zandra, heavily pregnant yet again, looked on laughing at Rafail's and Achilleas's toddling antics. Here at Anavolí, where Diamandis and Zandra had once done the same as children while their parents watched.

His family. His love. His heart.

He still had the picture of his parents that Zandra had given him in the hospital two years ago. He showed it to the boys often, so they would know the grandparents they'd never gotten to meet and the uncles they had been named after. He even spoke of them with Zandra, to the point where she felt like she did remember more than she had before.

He no longer let that old grieving love be a curse. He considered it part of all that love he was so lucky to have, every day.

Lysias handed his daughter over to Zandra and began to chase the boys so Katerina could take a break. She walked over to where Diamandis stood.

"It's a shame we have to head back tomorrow," she

said when she approached. "But it will be good to get back into a routine. The boys will be feral if we do not."

"I do not mind them feral."

His wife censured him with a sideways look. "Of course *you* do not," she said, making him chuckle.

She sighed, watching their boys, joy lighting her face. "You know, the doctor is quite certain it would be safe to try for more." She slid her arm around his waist and leaned into him.

He kissed her temple. "Whatever you wish, my queen."

And he would find a way, for all his years, to give her—to give their entire family—exactly that.

* * * * *

Were you captivated by
Pregnant at the Palace Altar?

*Then don't miss the first instalment in the
Secrets of the Kalyva Crown duet,*
Hired for His Royal Revenge!

*And why not check out Lorraine Hall's debut
for Harlequin Presents?*

The Prince's Royal Wedding Demand

Available now!

#4121 THE MAID MARRIED TO THE BILLIONAIRE
Cinderella Sisters for Billionaires
by Lynne Graham
Enigmatic billionaire Enzo discovers Skye frightened and on the run with her tiny siblings. Honorably, Enzo offers them sanctuary and Skye a job. But could their simmering attraction solve another problem—his need for a bride?

#4122 HIS HOUSEKEEPER'S TWIN BABY CONFESSION
by Abby Green
Housekeeper Carrie wasn't looking for love. Especially with her emotionally guarded boss, Massimo. But when their chemistry ignites on a trip to Buenos Aires, Carrie is left with some shocking news. She's expecting Massimo's twins!

#4123 IMPOSSIBLE HEIR FOR THE KING
Innocent Royal Runaways
by Natalie Anderson
Unwilling to inflict the crown on anyone else, King Niko didn't want a wife. But then he learns of a medical mix-up. Maia, a woman he's never met, is carrying his child! And there's only one way to legitimize his heir...

#4124 A RING TO CLAIM HER CROWN
by Amanda Cinelli
To become queen, Princess Minerva must marry. So when she sees her ex-fiancé, Liro, among her suitors, she's shocked! The past is raw between them, but the more time she spends in Liro's alluring presence, the more wearing anyone else's ring feels unthinkable...

#4125 THE BILLIONAIRE'S ACCIDENTAL LEGACY
From Destitute to Diamonds
by Millie Adams
When playboy billionaire Ewan "loses" his Scottish estate to poker pro Jessie, he doesn't expect the sizzling night they end up sharing... So months later when he sees a photo of a very beautiful, very *pregnant* Jessie, a new endgame is required. He's playing for keeps!

#4126 AWAKENED ON HER ROYAL WEDDING NIGHT
by Dani Collins
Prince Felipe must wed promptly or lose his crown. And though model Claudine is surprised by his proposal, she agrees. She's never felt the kind of searing heat that flashes between them before. But can she enjoy the benefits of their marital bed without catching feelings for her new husband?

#4127 UNVEILED AS THE ITALIAN'S BRIDE
by Cathy Williams
Dante needs a wife—urgently! And the business magnate looks to the one woman he trusts...his daughter's nanny! It's just a mutually beneficial business arrangement. Until their first kiss after "I do" lifts the veil on an inconvenient, inescapable attraction!

#4128 THE BOSS'S FORBIDDEN ASSISTANT
by Clare Connelly
Brazilian billionaire Salvador retreated to his private island after experiencing a tragic loss, vowing not to love again. When he's forced to hire a temporary assistant, he's convinced Harper Lawson won't meet his scrupulous standards... Instead, she exceeds them. If only he wasn't drawn to their untamable forbidden chemistry...

YOU CAN FIND MORE INFORMATION ON UPCOMING HARLEQUIN TITLES, FREE EXCERPTS AND MORE AT HARLEQUIN.COM.

HPCNMRB0623

Get 3 FREE REWARDS!

We'll send you 2 FREE Books _plus_ a FREE Mystery Gift.

FREE Value Over **$20**

Both the **Harlequin®** Desire and **Harlequin Presents®** series feature compelling novels filled with passion, sensuality and intriguing scandals.

HARLEQUIN
PLUS

Try the best multimedia
subscription service for romance
readers like you!

Read, Watch and Play.

Experience the easiest way to get
the romance content you crave.

Start your **FREE TRIAL** at
<u>www.harlequinplus.com/freetrial</u>.